THE PLEASURE BUSINESS

ALSO BY PATRICK ANDERSON

Novels

THE APPROACH TO KINGS

ACTIONS AND PASSIONS

THE PRESIDENT'S MISTRESS

FIRST FAMILY

LORDS OF THE EARTH

SINISTER FORCES

Nonfiction

THE PRESIDENTS' MEN

HIGH IN AMERICA

THE PLEASURE BUSINESS

A NOVEL BY

PATRICK ANDERSON

HARCOURT BRACE JOVANOVICH, PUBLISHERS

SAN DIEGO   NEW YORK   LONDON

Requests for permission to make copies of any part of the work should be mailed to: Copyrights and Permissions Department,
Harcourt Brace Jovanovich, Publishers, Orlando, Florida 32887.

Library of Congress Cataloging-in-Publication Data
Anderson, Patrick, 1936–
The pleasure business: a novel / by Patrick Anderson.—1st ed. p. cm.
ISBN 0-15-172047-9
I. Title.
PS3551.N377P5 1989
813'.54—dc19

Designed by Dalia Hartman
Printed in the United States of America

First edition

A B C D E

FOR LAURA
(AND SHANDY)

THE PLEASURE BUSINESS

1

It has been said that true happiness arrives when your last child leaves for college and the dog dies.

So it was for Linda and me.

Penny, our first, last, and only child, was down in Charlottesville, in her first semester at the University of Virginia. Rags III had two years earlier ascended to Cairn Heaven. Suddenly, thank God Almighty, we were free at last!

No more shouting matches about $200 phone bills. No more wrecked cars. No more sleepless nights when she didn't come home or bother to call. No more swarms of teenage locusts racing through our house, devouring food, booze, clothing, cosmetics, books, rugs, records, furniture, everything. No more noise and filth and confrontation and chaos—our baby was off to college, where hardened professionals could cope with her endless demands and irrational whims.

Her mother and I were at home, alone, engulfed by sweet, shimmering privacy, a peace that passeth understanding. We drove into Washington a few times that fall to see friends, the new Woody Allen movie, Sarah Vaughan at Blues Alley, but mostly we stayed in our country home, snug by our fire, reading, listening to good music (I was deep into Mozart and Louis Armstrong), and savoring the glorious stillness that had descended upon our lives.

Need I say that our paradise was soon to be lost?

It was in late October that she called, near the end of a spectacular autumn; the nights had grown chill, and Linda was starting to grumble about turning on the furnace.

"It's not for me," I muttered, engrossed in a new John Updike story in *The New Yorker*.

A second ring. Linda, curled up on the other end of our big green sofa, the end nearer the fire, did not deign to look up from her book. Linda had been threatening to reread Proust, and I (being afflicted with the idea that reading should be fun) had distracted her with a pile of vintage John D. MacDonald paperbacks. Once Linda met that old charmer Travis McGee, it was love at first sight; she hardly spoke to me anymore.

The phone rang a third time. I grumbled and heaved myself to my feet. What's a husband for if not to answer the phone while his wife sails the blue waters of Florida with Travis McGee? I shuffled into my study, silenced Mozart, and growled a hello.

"Collect from Penny—Will you pay?"

Pay? Of course I would pay. I'd been paying for eighteen years; why would I stop now? Actually, I had been threatening for weeks to stop accepting collect calls, but when the moment came, I always imagined my baby in jail or the hospital or some other jam that required a father's bold intervention.

"Hi, Daddy! What's up?"

Penny's jaunty greeting told me she was not in distress, only lonely and/or broke. In these first months of college she had been calling once or twice a day. It was an expensive habit, but endearing, too. Most of our friends' kids never called home.

"Not much, sweetie. Just a quiet evening by the fire."

"Do you miss me?"

"Constantly. What's up with you?"

"I'm really psyched. I got a B+ on my history paper."

"Good. How long did you work on it?"

"Well, I was at this party at Sigma Nu till four; then I drank about a gallon of coffee and wrote it before the class at ten."

I choked back words of good advice that would be politely ignored. The truth was, I used to churn out a lot of history papers by the dawn's early light. "So how's your social life? Any young princes on the scene?"

"I'm sort of going with three guys, but they're all jerks."

3

"There's a good one out there somewhere. Try looking in the library."

Penny hesitated, and I sensed that she was about to reach the heart of the matter, which almost certainly involved money. My daughter is a prodigious spender. Sometimes I have tried to tell her of my own college days—inspiring tales of toil and sacrifice—but she finds my early poverty irrelevant, indeed distasteful, just as she finds my present prosperity barely adequate to her needs.

Once again, she surprised me. "Can you talk?"

"Talk?"

"I mean, is Mommy there?"

"More or less. Why?"

"It's about Bonnie."

It took me a moment to realize she meant Bonnie Prescott. Bonnie's parents were old friends of ours; the two girls had grown up together.

"What about her?"

"Bonnie always liked you. She thinks you're cool."

"I am cool, sweetheart. So what about her?"

"She's, like, in trouble."

I eased shut the door of my study. "What kind of trouble?"

"I can't explain over the phone. Listen, are you still going to New York tomorrow to see your editor?"

"Right. My editor, my agent, and a couple of other great Americans."

"Mommy's not going with you?"

"You couldn't drag her to New York."

"See, the thing is, Bonnie's in New York, and she really needs to talk to you. I told her I'd call her back tonight and let her know."

"I thought she was at Princeton."

"She bagged Princeton."

I grew impatient. This conversation was costing me money, making my head hurt, and drawing me back into the dark swamp of teenage trauma, from whence I thought I had escaped.

"Penny, if she's in trouble, why doesn't she talk to her parents?"

"Oh, shit, Daddy."

I must explain that my lovely and cultivated daughter, who has been known to weep over lost puppies and sentimental poems, talks like a stevedore. She blames me for this affliction, claiming that I corrupted her innocent mind at a tender age. Which is, of course, a dirty fucking lie.

"You *know* she hates her parents," she continued. "That's what this is all about. Will you talk to her, Daddy? Please?"

We both knew the answer. "Tell her to call me at the Algonquin after lunch," I said with a sigh.

"Love you, Daddy!" my daughter cried, and as always the words made me melt a little. "Mommy, too."

"Love you, sweetheart." I replaced the phone,

revived Mozart, and returned to our living room. Linda glanced up from her book. "What was that all about?"

I poked the fire. "She got a B+ on her history paper. The boys are jerks."

I dislike deceiving Linda, in part because I'm no good at it. As novelists go, I'm a lousy liar. Still, years of living with two formidable women has taught me that my relationship with one of them must sometimes exclude the other—and, God knows, the two of them share a girl world that is a total mystery to me.

Linda joined me at the fire, stretching like a cat. "Young boys are always jerks," she said. "It's old codgers like you and McGee who're fun."

I know a come-on when I hear one. Linda, I should explain, is the sexiest woman alive. Her ears are sexy, her toes, the freckles on her back, every sweet inch of her. We nuzzled before the fire, then went up to bed where, once again, miracles unfolded, earthquakes, rainbows, shooting stars, supernatural forces lifting us up.

Would you believe, Dear Reader, that two people who've been sleeping together half their lives could suddenly find their sex life making a quantum leap from merely excellent to absolutely sensational?

If you're lucky, that's what happens when your child goes off to college and the dog dies.

2

Linda and I live in an old stone house on ten wooded acres in Loudoun County, Virginia, an hour's drive west of Washington. We have a creek in front of us, down by the road, a barn and a lake off to one side, and gentle hills all around.

We used to live in the District, but when my third novel made a bundle, we decided to move out where there were more trees and fewer muggers. Back in those days, Linda was a congressman's administrative assistant, one of the first women AAs on the Hill. She had a good salary, plenty of excitement, and a taste of the power that everyone in Washington supposedly lusts for. Then one day some good and wise men in New York agreed to pay $350,000 for the paperback rights to a thriller I'd written for the stated purpose of entertaining the reader and enriching the author.

That evening, somewhere during the second bottle of champagne, I said, "You know, we could move to the country except for your job."

Linda burped daintily, gave me an odd little smile, and unexpectedly burst into song: "Why don't you take this job and shove it!" I got the hint, and within weeks she had traded her glamorous political career for a new role as author's wife, farm manager, and full-time mother. She never looked back.

Dulles International, the world's most beautiful airport, is out our way, but there wasn't a convenient flight to New York the next morning, so I drove to Washington National to catch the old, reliable Eastern shuttle. The shuttle is costly and crowded, a cattle car for the high and mighty, but it's unexcelled for people watching. Diane Sawyer was aboard that morning (three points for her), and Crazy Al Haig and Sam Donaldson (I sat as far as possible from Sam, who may never fully recover from all those years spent bellowing at Reagan above the roar of a helicopter), and finally—dashing aboard just as they were closing the doors—the only potential president I can claim for a personal friend, Harrison Prescott.

I looked up from my *Times* when I heard someone call my name. There was Harry, moving gracefully down the narrow aisle, with a ferret-faced young aide running interference for him. I was genuinely glad to see him. Harry and I had drifted apart in recent years, but we went back a long way, and I was curious to know more about his unannounced campaign for president.

If you're my age, you have dim memories of one

indisputably great president, and you grew up under two or three other damn good ones; then, one bleak November day, some shots rang out in Texas, and ever since it has seemed our fate to be ruled by knaves and fools. Yet we still dream of again electing a president we can be proud of, and Harry Prescott was as likely a candidate as I saw on the horizon.

Harry has his faults—we'll get to those—but he combines a first-rate mind with charm, toughness, and underlying decency, and in twenty years in Washington I haven't known a dozen men I would say that about.

He touched my arm as he passed. "Catch you in a minute." With a wink he moved on, calling a big hello to Sam Donaldson as he went.

I should explain that Harry is the father of Bonnie, the girl whose supposed difficulties my daughter had called about the night before. To see Harry now was a coincidence, but not all that spectacular a coincidence; after two decades, you learn what a tight little island Washington is.

We and the Prescotts became neighbors in Cleveland Park in the early 1970s, when the girls were toddlers. In those days Harry was a Vietnam hero turned Senate aide, and soon enough he went home to the Northwest to run for the House, then, four years later, for the Senate, arriving in that august chamber at age thirty-six. Harry was one of the golden boys who make it all look easy.

It isn't easy, of course. To rise so far so fast, you make trade-offs, and they usually start at home. In Harry's case there was his wife, Amanda, who was rich and gorgeous and a world-class, five-star bitch. Amanda was Harry's one big mistake; he hadn't needed her millions, but at twenty-three they had looked too good to pass up. It's a mistake a lot of otherwise smart men make, and then pay for it for a long, long time.

Then there was Bonnie. God knows Harry loved her—loved her all the more because of Amanda's indifference to her—but running for Congress/Senate/President doesn't leave a lot of time for fatherhood. It's the old story. So, while we were living in Cleveland Park, Bonnie more or less grew up in our house, while Harry was out saving mankind and Amanda was conquering what is laughingly known as Washington society. (Society in Washington, like society in a Greyhound terminal, is somewhat transient.)

Even after we moved to the country and Amanda began shipping Bonnie off to boarding schools, she often turned up at our house during holidays, a gawky, winsome child who always looked lost. My Penny is tough as nails, and always has been, but Bonnie wasn't like that. Because she was raised by two powerful personalities, it had been her instinct to clam up, and who could blame her? I have a memory of Bonnie, age six or so, half-asleep in my lap, whispering, "I love you, Mr. Malloy," and me whispering back, "I

10

love you, Bonnie," and wondering if she ever heard those words at home.

So what had become of the sleepy little girl in my lap? I hadn't seen Bonnie in a couple of years, but I dimly remembered Penny describing her as "really wasted," or something that suggested drugs, and I wondered if that was what she wanted to talk about. Penny and I have always talked candidly about drugs. She tried most of them in her mid-teens—just as I've tried most of them over the years—and now, at eighteen, she's bored by them and has become a health-food nut.

I have a fatalistic view of parenthood. Half the battle is in the genes, I think, and you play the hand you're dealt. I see no reason to expect my daughter to be any more rational than I was at her age, or any less crazed by sex, drugs, and rock and roll.

Given this minimalist view of parenting, I've tried to focus on the essentials, like teaching my daughter to be honest, to care about sunsets and tennis and good chili, about Billie Holiday and Hank Williams and Louis Armstrong and Scott Fitzgerald and Shakespeare and Chaplin. In that area, at least, I hadn't done badly.

Anyway, if Bonnie had a drug problem and wanted a sympathetic ear, I would oblige. I unfolded my *Times* and was fuming about Bill Safire's column when Harry's aide appeared at my elbow.

"The senator wants to see you," he announced

unhappily. These bright young men fight hard for the boss's ear and do not surrender it gladly.

The young man took my seat, and I joined Harry in the smoking section. He was a good-looking man, not tall but powerfully built, with raven hair, a wide mouth, and a broken nose he was rather proud of—someone smashed him while he was scoring the winning touchdown for Yale in the Harvard game—The Game, I believe they call it.

He shook my hand warmly. "It's been too long, Grady," he said with that glowing smile of his, an oddly gentle, dreamy smile for such a tough, competitive man. I could have pointed out that except for Christmas cards we hadn't heard from him and Amanda for several years, but that would have been unkind. If you are a senator and running for president, you tend to focus on people who are of immediate value to you. Old friends are a luxury you may have to surrender in pursuit of the greater good.

"You've got all Washington on pins and needles, Harry," I said. It was a reference to Harry's status as an unannounced candidate for president. Half a dozen of his peers had tossed their hats in the ring and were barnstorming around America, shaking every hand and mounting every stump in sight. (One or two of them had been accused of mounting more than stumps and therefore had left the race, but that's another story.) But Harry held off announcing, playing the statesman, hoping the others would bloody each other; then he could waltz in and claim the nomination. It was a high-risk strategy; you had to admire his nerve.

Harry ignored my political snooping and asked, like any politician worth his salt, about my family. I told him about Linda's victories in Loudoun County politics and Penny's exploits in college. Harry complimented my latest novel—he tossed in a few specifics to prove he'd actually read it—and I told him about the movie deal.

It was disconcerting to talk to him. I have resented and resisted authority all my life, and yet I could not ignore the power that Harry represented. Power is like a fire in a cold, dark room; you're drawn to it by instinct. It warms you, flatters you, seduces you. At one level Harry was just a guy. We'd gotten drunk together, had violent arguments, shared crazy times. And yet he was not just a guy now—he was a potential president—and that made all the difference.

As we chatted, I thought about my daughter's call the night before. I could have said, "Harry, I'm seeing Bonnie today, she may have a problem, I'll let you know." But of course I couldn't say that. I had to play out the string, see the girl, then decide whether or not to talk to him. There are unspoken rules by which we live our lives; Harry and I were friends because, for all our differences, our instincts were much the same.

We were circling La Guardia when Harry got to

the point. "I'll announce after the first of the year, Grady. I've got a good shot. Right now I'm working on name recognition. I wish to hell you'd write some speeches for me."

Zap! There it was, the reason for all this concern and flattery, and I hadn't even seen it coming. I was annoyed, not at Harry but at myself, for being so naive.

"I don't see how I could," I told him. "I've started a new book. Besides, everyone knows you've got the best staff on the Hill."

Harry smiled serenely. He knew, as I did, that I hadn't said a flat, unequivocal I'd-rather-die-first no. "My staff's damn good," he conceded. "But they're young, issue-oriented. That's fine for the Senate, but you need more when you run for president. Hell, *you* know, Grady. You need themes, rhetoric, vision. My God, I remember those speeches you wrote."

He flattered me a bit more (stroked me, as the Nixon gang so nicely put it), recalling the time I'd written a celebrated "vision of America" speech for a candidate who actually became president. What no one had ever understood was that I wrote that speech tongue in cheek. *("I see an America with free love and nickel beer!")*

In truth, as far as I could perceive, my candidate's only true vision of America had been of himself enthroned in the White House and all the other politicians in the land lined up for miles along Pennsylvania

14

Avenue, begging for an opportunity to crawl into the Oval Office and kiss his ass.

"Couldn't you write for me part-time?" Harry asked. "Dammit, wouldn't you like to elect another president?"

He had me there, for Harry knew how I felt about my first campaign. It was the most extraordinary experience of my life, the ultimate ego trip, sort of a combination of bedding Miss America, pitching a no-hitter in the World Series, and winning World War III single-handedly.

"What's your consulting fee?" He thought he had me on the ropes now.

I laughed. "For you, old buddy, a piddling five hundred dollars a day plus an indoor parking space."

Harry winced; he's a tight man with a dollar. "The Senate can't pay a consultant that much." He sighed. "But I suppose CBA can." CBA was the Committee for a Better America, the "exploratory committee" that ran his shadowy campaign. "Then it's a deal?" he pressed.

I was tempted. My novel could wait. Fifteen years before, when we were neighbors, tennis partners, beer-drinking buddies, I'd have said yes in a minute. But I was annoyed by this burst of charm after years of silence, and I had too much money in the bank to be bulldozed. Fuck-you money, it's called. Old friend or not, Harry was a politician, and I've never met a politician who didn't hold you in contempt if you came cheap. "I'll think about it," I said as we touched down.

Harry had a limo waiting and insisted on giving me a ride to my hotel. We didn't talk on the way. His aide—Sid Katz was his name—briefed him on the municipal-bond market in anticipation of a luncheon with some Wall Street moguls, and I stared out at the moonscape of Queens, wondering as always if human life could survive there.

As we fought our way through the midtown traffic, Harry turned to me. "You know what's the worst thing about running for president?"

"Writing your own speeches?" I quipped.

"Raising money," he said impatiently. "You can't delegate it. The fat cats are spoiled. They expect you to come hat in hand. And you do. We all do. It's degrading, but there's no alternative the way the laws are now."

He stared out angrily at the chaos of Sixth Avenue. At that moment I liked him for his honesty and his anger. A moment later we stopped at the Algonquin. I climbed out, only to have Harry scoot out after me. He apparently had something he wanted to say away from Sid's prying ears. I wished to hell I'd caught another plane.

"There's something I should explain," he said. "You and Linda haven't heard from us in some time, and you deserve to know why."

That caught my attention. I'd wondered why their invitations had stopped. I have a tradition of drinking too much at Christmas parties, and I thought perhaps I'd said something that pissed Harry off.

"You know how Amanda is," he began.

I knew better than to respond to *that* one.

Harry's handsome face was pinched with pain. "Well, she got the idea there was something between Linda and me."

I laughed aloud. I couldn't help it. "You should be so lucky," I said.

"Thanks," he said bitterly. "Well, she got that bee in her bonnet and said she wouldn't see you two anymore. I just couldn't fight it. I should have spoken to you a long time ago— God knows it has nothing to do with how I feel about you and Linda."

I was amazed at how wrongheaded Amanda was, at how little she understood her husband, for Harry was one of the last men I would suspect of trying to hustle my wife. Yes, the womanizing senator is an American cliché, and not without cause, but there is another, quite different sort of politician, those so obsessed with the pursuit of power that they are all but asexual. Such men could be immensely sophisticated about politics, yet incredibly naive about women. Harry was a classic example. He might well be president in a couple of years, he knew the intricacies of all the feminist issues he would face, but everything he knew about real live women you could shove up a gnat's ass.

"Dammit, Grady, what can I say? I need you.

Just come write one speech. See how it feels. And you and I and Linda can have a good long lunch and get caught up."

I felt sorry for him; maybe that was what he intended. "Okay, Harry," I said. "Let's talk next week."

My friend the candidate grinned triumphantly—as always, he'd gotten what he wanted—and sped off to conquer Wall Street.

3

I was greeted at the Algonquin by a cordial "Welcome back, Mr. Malloy" from the desk clerk and bellmen. Twenty years before, on my first trips to New York, I'd rented a tiny second-floor room, right over the front entrance, for $16 a night. Now I commanded a $330 suite, with fresh flowers and a bottle of wine, compliments of the management. The elevators were ridiculously slow, and the days of the Round Table were long gone, but the Algonquin held warm memories, so I kept returning.

I arrived at the Four Seasons at one, but Fritz Hopper, my agent, was late, as he always is. I was on my second Bloody Mary when he arrived, circling the Grill Room like a shark, embracing various agents, editors, and TV tycoons. When he finally reached our table—his table—he peered at me suspiciously, as if he'd been expecting maybe Robert Redford or Steven Spielberg, and said accusingly, "Grady, you've put on weight."

19

"Thanks, Fritz," I sighed as a waiter, unbidden, poured his Perrier. Fritz had weighed 132 pounds forever.

We talked shop for a while. One of my early novels was inexplicably a best-seller in Japan. The film deal on another novel was in limbo because the wife of the director, a noted Malibu intellectual, had brought suit to prove he had gone mad. ("How could she tell?" I asked.) The most urgent issue was whether to accept a six-figure offer for my new novel from my current publisher or let Fritz shop it around.

"Those turkeys couldn't sell lemonade in hell," I groused. "Do your stuff."

That settled, Fritz treated me to some literary gossip while I busied myself eating and drinking everything in sight. Fritz skims off 10 percent of my income and just what he does for that money is debatable. He would say he has brilliantly masterminded my career, guiding me from obscurity to relative success. I sometimes think that all he does is draw up a boilerplate contract for each new book, make two or three phone calls, and rake in the dough. In any event, there is an unspoken agreement that once a year or so he owes me a world-class lunch. Thus, depending on your point of view, either he was graciously buying me a $100 lunch, or I had foolishly paid him tens of thousands of dollars for that $100 lunch.

You must understand that writers are the poor

relations of the otherwise elegant world of publishing. We are forever embarrassing everyone, for we persist in showing up ill-dressed and uncouth, often creating scenes in the best restaurants, raving that we have bills to pay and children to educate. Our long-suffering agents and editors know that all they can do is get us drunk and ship us back to whatever squalid place we came from in hopes we'll return to our word processors and thus justify our short, nasty, brutish lives.

In time a waiter brought the dessert cart, and I almost cried. I thought I'd died and gone to Calorie Heaven. Fritz doesn't eat dessert, of course, so I ordered two while he smiled indulgently; he is fond of saying that all writers are children. When I finished my desserts, washed down by a double brandy, Fritz signed the check and hurried off to meet his mistress, as he does every afternoon, while desperate writers try to reach him on the phone. Meanwhile, I returned to the Algonquin, flopped into bed, and sank into the deepest of sleeps.

I might be sleeping still had not the phone rung in the early evening. I groped for it in the autumn dusk, still too besotted to be sure where I was, and was confounded by the cheerful voice that said, "Mr. Malloy? It's me!"

"Huh? Wha'?"

"Me! Bonnie! Didn't Penny tell you?"

The previous night's conversation came back

slowly, like a dream. This was Bonnie Prescott, a child I hadn't seen in too many years but who somehow needed my help.

I asked her to meet me in the Blue Bar in an hour.

Among my vices is punctuality. I showered, dressed—Guccis, gray flannels, my best brown tweed coat, a knit tie—and was settling myself on a barstool in precisely sixty minutes, groggy but game. Bonnie wasn't there, of course, but I didn't care. The tiny Blue Bar is one of my favorite spots in New York. Linda and I discovered it on our first trip to New York two decades before, and it was good to recall those days when we were young and poor and quite addled by love. I was your basic dreams-of-glory reporter then, rising before dawn to bang out my first novel and imagining myself the next Scott Fitzgerald. That was not precisely how it turned out, but I had no complaints.

The bartender proved to be an aspiring actor, and we were soon deep into a discussion of John Guare's plays. Then, as the bar filled up, he no longer had time to talk. Bonnie was more than an hour late, but I understand the ways of teenage girls; it has been said of my Penny, not unfairly, that she could fuck up a junkyard. I sipped my drink and thought about a novel I wanted to write, and soon I was oblivious to the Blue Bar and the Algonquin and all of New York. I don't know how much time had passed when I felt a hand on my arm.

22

"Hi, Mr. Malloy."

The voice was hesitant, gentle as moonlight.

I turned and saw a young woman I barely recognized. The Bonnie I remembered was a skinny beanpole, all long legs and skinned elbows, with a ponytail and braces on her teeth. This creature struck me as one of the most beautiful women in New York. She was tall and slender, with a pale oval face, sad dark eyes, a pouty ruby-red mouth, and a glorious crown of bobbed platinum hair. She looked like what Marilyn would have looked like if she'd been eighteen and cover-girl tall and thin.

She was dressed simply but stylishly in boots, designer jeans, a pickle-green silk blouse, and a white jacket. I smiled and took her hand and gazed into her large, unblinking eyes and found myself quite unnerved; beautiful women do that to me. "You've grown up, Bonnie," I murmured.

But she was already speaking.

". . . sorry I'm late, but I had this fight with my landlord and it's been such a hassle and now I need to see my friend Monica—she's so neat, you'll love her—because she owes me some money, then there's this really hot club we could go to . . ."

Something was wrong. Her looks were serene but her words frenetic. She was a lovely picture that wasn't quite in focus. Looking back, I guessed Bonnie had always been a little vague, a little out of it, in a sweet way, but this seemed something more. Drugs?

I assumed it would all come out in time, so we took a cab uptown to see someone really neat called Monica.

Our destination proved to be a shining tower on First Avenue. While I paid the driver, Bonnie dashed ahead of me into the building. She pranced like a colt; she was so beautiful you forgot how young she was. In the lobby, she greeted a Puerto Rican security guard who was playing solitaire. "Hey, Buzzo, what's up?"

The boy muttered that everything was cool.

"Red jack on the queen," Bonnie said. "You want to tell Monica I'm here?"

"Surprise her." The boy shrugged and listlessly played the jack.

Bonnie skipped to the elevators. As we shot up to the thirty-third floor, she took my arm and whispered, "Everyone here calls me Blair. I think Bonnie's so juvenile, don't you?"

If Bonnie was my young Marilyn, the thirtyish champagne blonde who opened the door of 33-B was Veronica Lake, sleek as a gull in a white pantsuit. "Monica!" Bonnie cried. The blonde allowed herself to be embraced but all the while kept one cool green eye on me.

"This is Grady," Bonnie announced, smoothly shifting gears after a lifetime of "Mr. Malloy."

"Hello, Grady." Monica brushed my palm with cool fingertips. "Do come in. A few people are . . . having a drink." I thought I heard echoes of the Southwest, perhaps Texas, in her languid voice.

24

Monica's apartment was quite grand. The far wall was two stories high and all glass, with a dramatic view of the East River. There were white marble fireplaces at either end of the room, a Calder mobile floating overhead, and black leather chairs clustered around chrome-and-glass coffee tables. The look of the place was high-tech; Miles Davis's "Kind of Blue" floated from a state-of-the-art sound system, but was softened by huge vases of fresh flowers, Oriental rugs, and the blazing Chagall tapestries that graced one wall. The crowning, Busby Berkeley touch was a boldly lit spiral staircase that floated up to a balcony and God knows what sweet delights beyond.

Alas, there were people, too, gathered around one of the coffee tables. Monica guided us in that direction. By then I had her pegged for a Houston oil heiress.

Bonnie raced ahead like an eager puppy. "Hi, guys, I'm Blair! Remember me?"

Three gorgeous young women were sitting on the floor; one of them wore a T-shirt that said "So Many Men" across the front. I didn't get the joke until she hugged Bonnie and I saw "So Little Time" on the back.

There were three men, too, sitting on the sofas; I took them to be Arabs. One was in his early twenties, and rather pretty, with his smooth olive skin, liquid brown eyes, and fine-boned face. He wore a Savile Row suit and a world-weary expression. The other two were older, thicker, and wore suits off the rack.

All three eyed me disdainfully and Bonnie lustfully.

"I met you here before," Bonnie said to the young one. "You're Ahmad, right? Where's your brother? Oh, this is my friend Grady."

The lad did not leap up to embrace me. I glanced at him and his pals a moment, drawled, "Real nice to meet you fellows," and wandered off in search of refreshment.

Monica and Bonnie followed me to the bar. The view truly was sensational. New York always looks better at night. Monica poured champagne—the house wine, it seemed—and asked, "Are you a New Yorker, Grady?"

"I live in Virginia."

"Is it pleasant there?"

"As green and lovely as your eyes."

"You *are* a charmer. What brings you to our fair city?"

"Business," I said. "I'm a writer."

I've known women to be interested, even intrigued, by my profession, but Monica reacted as though I'd proclaimed myself a thrill killer. Her pretty face hardened, and she looked daggers at Bonnie, who, oblivious to her friend's anger, was chattering about her troubles with her landlord.

Just then, an ungodly howl filled the room. We all looked up—the commotion seemed to come from above—and the two burly Arabs jumped to their feet and reached inside their coats. It was then I realized they were armed.

Another handsome young Arab, perhaps the brother of the first one, was leaning over the balcony. He was wrapped in a sheet and laughing his fool head off. The hand that wasn't clutching the sheet was waving a bottle of champagne. A blonde in a shimmering robe stood behind him, her arms around his waist. Clearly, upstairs was the place to be.

The lad in the sheet let out another Tarzan howl; he was out of his skull. He jabbered in his native tongue; then the young one downstairs stood up, took a silver gadget out of his pocket, and flung it through the air. The one upstairs, juggling the champagne neatly, speared the gadget with one hand, jabbered a bit more, then disappeared down the hallway with the blonde.

The youth on the sofa cut his dark eyes toward Monica. "We need more cocaine."

Monica still looked pissed. "Blair, could I speak to you a moment?" she said, and they slipped away.

I was starting to enjoy myself. I spend most of my time in a small room, dealing in fantasies, so it is always a treat to explore the real world. Reality is a nice place to visit, but I wouldn't want to live there.

Not wanting to miss anything, I drifted over and took a seat beside the sleek young Arab. He had another of the silver gadgets in his hand, and he offered it to me, but with an ironic smirk, as if I were clearly too much of a dolt to comprehend it. In fact, I've done cocaine a few times, but never in the company of strangers. "No thanks, *amigo*."

"I want some." It was the girl in the "So Many Men" T-shirt. I had by then lost interest in what was on her T-shirt, being dumbfounded by what was in it; the girl was nobly proportioned. The youth ignored her, as he'd been ignoring the three women since I arrived. "What a bunch of creeps," one of the girls muttered.

"What do you fellows do?" I asked, too loudly to be ignored.

The young one gave me a look, then said in his clipped English, "We spend much money to support your great nation." They all had a giggle on that, and I was framing a suitable reply when Monica and Bonnie returned, on the tail end of an argument.

"I'm *counting* on you," Monica said heatedly.

"I'll *think* about it," Bonnie shot back.

Bonnie touched my shoulder. "Grady, they've got plans; maybe we'd better go."

"Don't rush off," the young Arab said, and his two burly baby-sitters chortled with delight.

I stood up. "Great to meet you boys," I said. I whistled a few bars of "The Sheik of Araby," too, as Monica guided us to the door, but I doubt if they got it.

"Such a pleasure to meet you," Monica said, cool as lemonade again.

"You have interesting friends."

She showed teeth like a string of pearls. "If you only knew."

In the elevator, Bonnie clutched my arm. "A charming bunch," I said.

"The Arabs are such pigs!" she said with sudden passion. "They have so much money they think they can come to our country and treat everybody like dirt. The thing is, the Arab king, he has, like, a hundred sons, royal princes, and they all fight and scheme, and sometimes people get kidnapped or murdered, so their parents send them over here and give them bags of money for women and drugs and gambling, and then when it's safe, they go back home. They think they're such hot stuff, and they're just pigs. They *hate* women, just *hate* us."

It was all coming too fast for me. In the lobby, I asked, "Were those guys princes?"

"The two young ones. The others were body-guards." She waved absently at Buzzo, the security guard, who was still losing his game of solitaire.

A cab stopped as we neared the curb. A lucky break, I thought, until I saw the character who climbed out. He was the size of a barn, with coffee-colored skin, a sleek black beard, and dark eyes that burned with pure malevolence. First you saw his size—that

29

brute body straining beneath the well-cut dark suit and cashmere overcoat—and then you felt the cold, sinister aura of the man. There was no reason to fear him on a busy city street, and yet the sight of him made me shiver. I took Bonnie's arm as I realized that he was blocking our path, a nasty smirk on his face.

"Where you been, kid?" His voice was gruff and menacing.

"Just around, Nicky," she said in a tiny, frightened whimper. We were frozen there for a moment. It was like confronting a mountain. I was immobilized by confusion and shock. Who was this ape, and how did Bonnie know him?

"You come see me, okay?"

"Sure, Nicky," she whispered. Then the guy marched past us, and we slipped into the cab. I gave the driver the address of Orso's, a Times Square restaurant, then slumped in the seat, trying to collect my thoughts. Bonnie huddled beside me, trembling, clutching my arm, her head on my shoulder.

"Who was that guy?" I asked as our cab entered Central Park.

"His name is Nicky Allegro. He's taking some coke to Ahmad. See, there'll be more Arabs coming, and they'll need lots of coke."

I felt her body tremble. "Oh, God, I hate them; I hate them all," she said, sobbing.

I let her cry. I was thinking hard about Monica and the Arabs and the cocaine—the whole bizarre, ugly scene—and I was angry and confused that Bonnie would know such people.

Our cab neared my restaurant. I squeezed Bonnie's hand. "Listen, beautiful, I'm going to buy you a great pizza, and you're going to tell Uncle Grady what the hell's going on. Okay?"

She bit her lip and nodded. The cab stopped, and I took her arm and led her into Orso's.

I ordered pizza and wine, then caught Bonnie's eye and wouldn't let go. She tried to smile, and it hurt us both, and when she spoke, I could barely hear her over the clatter of the restaurant.

"I've been having dates with men."

I puzzled over that one and finally said, "Well, that's normal."

"For money."

I'm slow, but I do catch on. "You mean . . ."

She began to nod, her eyes huge and heartbreaking.

". . . having sex for money?"

"Monica's sort of a madam. I mean, that's a silly thing to call it, but all these rich men come to town, not just Americans, Arabs and Japanese and Italians, whatever, and they call Monica, and she gets girls to, like, entertain them. They'll pay Monica five hundred dollars just for a regular date, and the girl gets half.

It's easy to make a thousand dollars a week, two thousand if you want to."

She sipped her wine and gazed at me through her long, tangled lashes. Maybe she was trying to gauge my reaction. I tried to be deadpan, but I didn't feel that way inside. In the first gut-wrenching moment, I felt as if the girl I'd known, the one I'd bounced on my knee and watched grow up, had been murdered. But she hadn't. She was sitting there, lovely and loopy and inscrutable, awaiting my response.

I thought of a dozen questions but settled on Old Reliable: "Bonnie, how did this get started?"

She brightened; she wanted to tell her story more than I wanted to hear it. "Grady—you don't mind if I call you Grady?"

"No."

"I must have told Penny a million times how lucky she was to have you for a father. All her girlfriends were in love with you, you and Mrs. Malloy, too. You gave her space to grow, so no matter how wild Penny got, she always loved you."

It was the kind of compliment that makes you want to cry, but I just waited. When she pulled a cigarette from her purse, I softened a little and lit it for her.

She blew out smoke. "How did it start? I guess it really started a long time ago when I figured out I wasn't a genius like my father or a queen of society like my mother. I was just me, but they wouldn't accept that. All through boarding school, it was, What about your grades? What about your SATs? How will you ever get into a decent college? What are you going to do with your life? Blah blah blah. Finally, Daddy moved mountains to get me into Princeton, and it was filled with the same obnoxious preppies I was sick of, so I bagged it. I went home and very politely said it wasn't working out and maybe I could go to art school somewhere."

She puffed on her cigarette, one-two-three times; I noticed a couple across the room staring at us.

"I really do like to draw, Grady. It's the only thing I've ever been any good at. The year I was at Foxcroft, I had a really super art teacher who encouraged me, and that's what I want to do, go to art school, not mess with science and languages and all those things I'm no good at.

"But when I tried to tell my parents how I felt, they freaked out. How could I disgrace them like this? Actually, it was mostly my mother. 'You'll never get another dime from us,' she said. 'That's cool,' I told her. 'I don't want another dime from you.' She always came back to money; it was emotional blackmail. We give you all this money, so why don't you do what we want? I couldn't stand it any longer. I had to stop taking their money or I'd never be free.

"So I just walked out the door with nothing but the clothes on my back and thirty dollars in my pocket and hitchhiked to New York. I met some kids in the Village and got a job waitressing, and it was fun, except that I was living in this real dump with about ten other people. Then I met Annette."

Our pizza arrived. It had the thinnest, crispest crust imaginable. We had a bite; then I said, "Annette?"

"Right. She had this neat apartment in the Village, and she invited me to stay with her. She was really cool—she was there tonight, with the T-shirt on—and it was great. But after a while I got curious. I mean, Annette didn't work, but she always had plenty of money and dressed nice and bought my meals if we ate out. Finally, I asked her what her secret was, and she told me about Monica."

She nibbled at her pizza until I prompted her again.

"Monica fixed Annette up with dates. She'd get two-fifty each time, and big tips, and she just did it when she felt like it. So she asked if I wanted to meet Monica."

She sipped her wine. "Boy, this is great pizza."

"So you met Monica?"

"I was curious. We went up to her apartment one afternoon, and Monica hugged me and said, 'Oh, she's perfect, the girl next door, men will love her!' It was sort of flattering, I guess. We had drinks, and maybe did some coke, and she just begged me to come back the next Saturday night, when these Japanese guys were coming by, big shots from one of the car companies. So I told her I'd think about it."

"And what did you think?"

"Honestly, I thought it sounded like winning the lottery. I mean, I'm eighteen, sex is no big deal, and waitressing is really murder after a while. I guess I was greedy. I thought I could get my own apartment and go to art school and be on my own. I'd found out what it was like to be broke, and a thousand dollars a week sounded too cool to be true."

"So you went that Saturday night?"

"This Japanese guy, I guess he was fifty, and he was so polite it was funny. I mean, I had a couple of drinks first, and the whole thing was over in twenty minutes, and then he bowed and said, 'Thank you,' and I went home with three hundred and fifty dollars. It wasn't anything. I was like an actress playing a part. When I left, I went to a bar and picked up the prettiest boy there and forgot all about Mr. Himoshima, or whatever his name was."

I like to think that I'm worldly-wise, that nothing shocks me, but I was having a hard time accepting that this cynical, sordid story was coming from the lips of this sweet, sad child. She looked so damn lovely and innocent.

"Bonnie, how many times have you done this?"

She shrugged, eyes downcast. "Not a whole lot.

Not nearly as much as Monica wants me to. Just enough for rent and spending money."

I shoved my pizza away and asked our waitress for a brandy. "Bonnie, don't tell me you're doing this because you need the money. I'll write you a check, right now, for all the money you want. I don't think you know why you're doing it. Do you want to hurt your parents? Do you want them to find out? You must know what this could do to your father."

"No! I don't want to hurt them, honest. I just want to be free of them. My mother is such an impossible bitch, and my father, God, he's a sweet man, but he's just so far out of it. I mean, my father thinks I'm still a virgin. The thing is, Monica is my best friend up here, and—"

"Bullshit!" I yelled. "The bitch is selling your flesh and taking half the money. That's no friend."

"No, you don't understand."

The couple across the room was staring at us again. I muttered something nasty in their direction, then lowered my voice. "Bonnie, don't you realize what could happen? You could be arrested. You could catch AIDS, for Christ's sake. Some madman could beat you up or kill you. And you could mess up your head in ways you can't even imagine. For God's sake, believe me, you're better off as a waitress or coming to terms with your parents or anything. You've got to stop this before it's too late."

She nibbled the last of her pizza and reached for mine. "I know," she said with a little sigh. "I do want to stop. That's why I told Penny I wanted to talk to you. Because you're a writer and a friend and such a nice man. I thought that was the perfect answer, you know, that you and I together, we could, you know, make so much money if we . . ."

She gave me a bright, expectant smile. Once again I was entirely lost. "We could what, Bonnie?"

She gave me a dazzling smile. "We could write a book," she explained.

5

I almost fell out of my chair. Was this how far we had sunk in media-mad America? Did this child of the video age dream of appearing masked on "Good Morning America"? Did she imagine her sad story as a "Movie of the Week"? I busied myself with the check, and to gain time, I suggested that we walk back to the Algonquin.

The hell of it was, I realized as we pushed through the inferno of Times Square, it could probably be done. She had a story to tell, I knew how to tell it, and Fritz Hopper could surely find a publisher. If it could be done anonymously, maybe she could take the money and start a new life. Maybe, besides the money, telling her story would be a catharsis, a way of putting the whole mess behind her. I didn't know; I was groping. I only knew I wanted to keep her trust until I found a way to rescue her.

The Algonquin was packed with the after-theater crowd. We could hear Julie Wilson singing

"Bewitched, Bothered and Bewildered" in the Oak Room. I found us a sofa in the corner of the lobby where we could talk in privacy. When we were settled, she batted her eyes at me and said, "What do you think of my idea?"

What did I think? Part of me, the part that is pure writer and thus perfectly amoral, thought it was a hell of a story, one I'd love to tell. But another part of me, the part that keeps a faint grip on reality, was yelling that it was ridiculous to think I could write about how Harry Prescott's daughter dabbled as a call girl.

"It might work," I told her. "We'd have to change the details—make you a doctor's daughter from Chicago, say. But I wouldn't consider it, Bonnie, unless you stop what you're doing."

She nodded wistfully. I wondered what people thought of us. That she was a schoolgirl and I her father? I doubted that even the most jaded New Yorker would guess we were discussing a book on her career as a high-priced hooker.

"Would it help," she said, "if I told you some, you know, specifics?"

I gulped. She started to talk. I guided her with an occasional question. She said she knew dozens of young women doing what she had done. A lot of them "got messed up on drugs," but smart ones, like Monica, had more business than they could handle. Soon they were calling in friends to help and looking for a bigger apartment in a better neighborhood. That was what Monica had done. She might still turn a trick with a few favored clients, but essentially she was a busy executive, juggling supply and demand, men who wanted sex and women who wanted money.

She told her story nonchalantly, with no bitterness, with even flashes of humor, and yet I still felt that something was wrong, that she was dazed, off center.

Bonnie had mentioned that Monica's clients included Arabs and Japanese, and I asked if she dealt exclusively in foreigners. "No, plenty of Americans come, too, businessmen and editors and movie stars, all kinds. But the foreigners are great because they've got so *much* money and they really don't want any hassle."

She told me about other "madams" she'd met. One she called Ruth ran an upscale real estate office; another managed an East Side boutique. Some madams had girls living in their apartments. "It's practically slavery. They have all these rules, and they charge the girls every time they drink a Pepsi or anything, and some of them push cocaine on the girls so they end up working for drugs."

It sounded as if Bonnie, because she was young and lovely, had quickly become a hot item; everyone wanted her services. Men often wanted to make dates directly. That meant more money—it eliminated the madam and her percentage—but it also meant danger, venturing into unknown places with unknown people.

"Most of the men are really nice, a lot nicer than the guys you meet in bars," she insisted. "They're just lonely. Lots of them are gay, or afraid they are. Or getting old and unhappy about, you know, losing it. There's one man who loves to take me shopping and buy me pretty lingerie. I think he really wishes he could buy it for himself."

"It's so strange," she added. "These men are rich and famous, but sex gives you such power over them."

It was, I thought, a perverted, even pathetic "power," but I didn't argue. Engrossed in her story, I hadn't noticed as the lobby thinned out until we were the last people left. I yawned and stood up. Bonnie gave me a funny look and said, "Do you want to talk some more?"

"Do you?"

"It's weird, but to talk about it really helps me understand what I've been doing. Does that make sense?"

"Sure," I told her. "We'll find someplace we can get coffee."

"Maybe we could go up to your room," she said. "I need to use the bathroom, anyway."

We took the elevator up. I found some classical music on the radio while she was in the bathroom. When she emerged, she stretched out on the sofa, her long legs extended, giggling, fluttering her toes at the ceiling. I wondered if she'd done coke in there.

"Where were we?" she asked.

I wasn't sure, but I had a question. "That big guy we saw tonight, the cocaine dealer, how does he fit in all this? Nicky Allegro, is that what you called him?"

It was as if I'd hit her. She turned away from me and curled into a ball. I thought she was trembling. I listened to Beethoven playing softly until she said, "I don't think I can talk about him."

"Okay," I said. "Forget it. It doesn't matter."

She turned and faced me, suddenly a small, frightened child. "No, I've got to tell you the truth. It hasn't all been fun and games. I met Nicky at Monica's a couple of times. He was always talking about the great parties he had and how I should come to one. But I didn't want to—he scares me—and then one night he was talking about this big party he was giving and how Billy Idol would be there. So finally I said okay, I'd come by. Well, Billy Idol wasn't there. You know who was there? Dealers. All these thugs with, like, suitcases full of cocaine, all these Colombians, really bad people. And a lot of real cheap women. As soon as I got there, I wanted to leave, but they wouldn't let me leave. At first it was a joke, but then it wasn't a joke anymore. They kept me there . . . did things to me. They kept me there two nights, until Monica came and made Nicky let me go."

She began to sob. "I can't talk about it, Grady. I really can't."

I took her hand and listened to Beethoven and thought of stories about white women who were kidnapped by Indians in the nineteenth century and how, after a few years, even if they were rescued, it was too late for them to return to their own people. Bonnie was young, and I thought she could be saved, yet I feared that if she stayed much longer in this cruel and violent world, she would be lost.

"Bonnie, I'm sorry," I said. "So sorry."

She looked at me and wiped away her tears. "You want to hear something crazy? That wasn't the worst thing that ever happened to me. It was the second worst. You want to hear the worst?"

"No."

"It's okay. It's a different sort of worst. When I first started going to Monica's, I used the money to get an apartment in the Village, but I was never there. People could never reach me. So finally I got a beeper—you know, like doctors have? Well, about that time I met this really sweet boy. He lived in the Village, too. He really *lived* there; his parents own a little restaurant. We started hanging out together, going for walks, just a friendship. He thought I was a college girl; he was sort of in awe of me.

"One night we went out to dinner. It was very romantic; there were candles, and he was holding my hand, but in the middle of dinner my beeper went off. I called and it was Monica and she had an emergency, some Israeli politicians or something, and I had to come help her out. It was awful. I really owed her a favor, so I told Mike—his name was Mario but I always called him Mike—I had to go uptown for a couple of hours but maybe I could meet him later. Even when I said it it sounded terrible— I mean, he was not a stupid person. I didn't hear from him for a few days, so I went to see him, but he wouldn't talk to me, didn't want anything to do with me. And I couldn't blame him.

"Do you understand, Grady? I liked him a lot— he was the nicest boy I ever met—but I lost him because of this crazy thing I'm doing. And that's the worst thing that's happened to me."

I didn't know what to say. My emotions were all gone, and my curiosity, too. I stood up. "You'd better go. Maybe we can talk again tomorrow."

She went into the bathroom again. I pulled off my tie and tossed it over a doorknob. When Bonnie came out, she'd washed her face and brushed her hair.

"I saw your father today," I said.

"How is he?"

"He's running for president. He wants me to write speeches for him."

"Poor Grady, everybody wants you to write for them." She smiled sadly and added, as if it were an afterthought, "The thing is, I don't have anyplace to go."

I was lost again.

"It's like I said, I loaned my apartment to some

45

kids when I was in L.A. last week. They must have had some pretty wild parties because my landlord locked me out. That's what I was doing today, looking for an apartment. So I don't have anyplace to go, except maybe Monica's."

She came and put her arms around me, and I held her close and felt how fragile, how vulnerable, she was and wondered what the hell I could do for her. Then she kissed me, and it wasn't a little-girl kiss, wasn't even close. When I broke it off, she looped her fingers in my belt and gave me a pitiful, lost-puppy look. "Maybe I could stay here."

I won't pretend I wasn't tempted. Yet even as I was drawn by her youth and beauty and sadness, I heard the alarms going off. She had spoken of the power that sex gave her over men. God knows she needed love, perhaps she even needed a place to stay, but I feared that was not all of it. I feared it was her instinct to use sex to increase her power over me; she knew all too well what fools sex can make of men my age. She had, after all, two parents who were, in their different ways, subtle and domineering people; to manipulate others was in her genes. She had said that as a call girl she was only an actress playing a role, and I didn't know what role she was playing now or what part she wanted me to play in her drama.

This much I know: My decision had nothing to do with morality and everything to do with self-preservation. If I'd done what she wanted, she'd have had me in the palm of her sweet little hand, and that was not where I wished to be.

"You're a lovely girl, Bonnie, but it's not a good idea. I'll get you a room in the hotel if you want one, but for you to stay here would only cause problems."

She gave me a long, wistful look, and I was wavering when abruptly she kissed me and slipped out the door. She didn't say where she was going, and I didn't ask.

I met with editors for breakfast, midmorning coffee, and lunch the next day. We kicked around various book ideas. I mentioned to each editor that I knew an articulate teenager from a good family who'd been working as a call girl and might tell her story anonymously.

The first editor, as decent a woman as could be found in the depraved world of publishing, looked pained and said, "Oh, Grady, it sounds so sordid!"

The second, a gentleman of the most dazzling sophistication, murmured, "Really, Grady, there are so many tarts to be found, aren't there?"

The third, a pleasantly plump woman with teen-age daughters of her own, cried, "Oh, God, it's every mother's nightmare!" and begged me to put something on paper.

So much for the theory that all editors think the same.

There the matter rested until I boarded the shuttle

home that afternoon. Aloft, I returned to my senses. Perhaps it was being free of the gravitational pull of Manhattan, or perhaps it was being surrounded by all those cold-eyed lawyers, but I realized there was no way in hell I could write about Bonnie no matter how we fuzzed her identity.

It might have been possible if she'd been a stranger to me, but this was *Harry Prescott's daughter*. How long would she be anonymous? Could I trust an unstable, coked-up teenager to keep a secret? And what would Harry do when he found out? Probably dig out one of those bayonets he brought home from Vietnam and slice me limb from limb. And who would blame him?

My duty, clearly, was to lure Bonnie back to reality, not to become enmeshed in her fantasies. Books are books, and life is life, and it is sometimes necessary for even a professional writer to distinguish between them. The question I pondered as I winged homeward was how I could disentangle Bonnie from this mess with the least possible harm to her and everyone else. With a groan I realized that Bonnie's mess had become my mess, too.

Linda was out in the yard raking leaves, wearing her tan corduroy pants, a faded red plaid shirt, and an old pair of sneakers. Some ducks were paddling about our pond, the sun was setting behind the hill, and our little world was so quiet and beautiful that I wanted to cry. Instead, I kissed her, and she put her hands in my hair and kissed me back. Then the phone rang inside the house, and like a fool, I went and answered it.

It was Penny, collect, and the first thing she said was "Did you talk to Bonnie?"

"Yeah, I talked to her."

"How was she?"

"How the hell do you think? She's doing something crazy and dangerous that could screw up her whole life. You could have warned me, you know."

"I started to, Daddy. But I decided you'd better see for yourself. It's all so gross. Did you talk about a book?"

"Yeah."

"Will you do it?"

"No, dammit, no! It's insane."

"It might sell a million copies. And you could give me ten percent, since it was my idea."

"Go to law school, sweetheart. You'll make a wonderful lawyer."

"So what are you going to do?"

"I'm going to try to help her."

"The thing is, Bonnie doesn't have a real tight grip on reality. When things get bad, she does a lot of coke and just floats. And sometimes she's sort of suicidal. You won't tell her parents, will you?"

"I should. She's their responsibility. But it's hard to see how they could help now."

"They can't. Her mother is really awful. When Bonnie said she wouldn't go to college, her mother threatened to have her *committed*. What a flaming bitch!"

"I asked Bonnie to call me in a couple of days. I want to see if I can find her a job in Washington."

At that point I was glad Penny had called. I was feeling pretty proud of myself, the Good Samaritan. Then she said, "Well, let me know what happens. If you can't convince her, I'll go see her and try."

"*What?*" I yelled. "Dammit, you stay away from her. It's dangerous up there."

Her reply was soft, inevitable. "Daddy, she's my friend."

And there it was. Bonnie was her friend.

The thought of Penny entering Bonnie's mad world filled me with terror. But Penny wouldn't see it that way. My daughter has many qualities I admire and some I regret, but she has few emotions stronger than her loyalty to the girls who are her friends. At eighteen, they've survived so much together—broken hearts and abortions and drugs and family battles and fancy prep schools and the college-admissions ordeal—that they are fiercely loyal, a sisterhood with vows signed in blood and tears. If Penny thought Bonnie needed her help, she'd go to New York—she'd storm the gates of hell—and all I could do was try to make the visit unnecessary.

The next morning, Linda and I shared a leisurely Sunday in bed. She was conquering the *Washington Post*'s crossword puzzle, and I had settled down with the book-review section. Then the phone rang.

I answered it and heard the screams, wild, anguished cries of fear and pain; it might have been a hot line to hell. My blood froze as I recognized her, and then she whispered, "Daddy?"

"Baby, what is it?"

She kept crying and sobbing, and I shouted, "Penny, get control of yourself! What is it?"

Linda was beside me, clutching my arm. Finally, Penny said, "Have you seen the *New York Times*?"

"Today's *Times*? No."

"Oh, God, get it! Read the story on the front page, then call me back. Daddy, I'm scared!"

She hung up. Linda said, "What is it?"

"I'll be back," I said, and soon I was speeding toward the home of our neighbor Elton Capps, who drove into Leesburg every Sunday morning to pick up the *Times*. Then I was in his kitchen, staring dumbly at the headline that had plunged Penny into hysterics:

ARABS, YOUNG WOMEN SLAIN
IN EAST SIDE APARTMENT

POLICE SAY MASS MURDER
MAY BE DRUG RELATED

The story listed the names of the four dead Arabs. One, whose age was given as twenty-two, was Ahmad Faisal, and I took that to be the boy I'd met. The others were men in their forties whose names meant nothing to me; one was described as "a prominent Saudi businessman."

One of the women was listed as Monica Wilcox, twenty-seven, a model, originally of Dallas. The story said the identities of the two other women hadn't been established. It said that all seven had been bound and shot in the back of the head, execution style.

"Grady, what is it?" my friend was asking. Elton was a retired CIA official, a smart man, a good friend, but I couldn't answer. I left without a word. There was no doubt that this was Monica's apartment, that Monica was dead, and possibly one or more of the Arabs I'd seen the week before. The unanswered question was whether Bonnie was one of the two unidentified women; Penny must have known Monica's name and recognized that possibility at once.

I drove back home and told Linda that I'd seen Bonnie when I was in New York. "We went for a drink with a friend of hers. It was the same apartment where these people were killed. I've got to go up there, right away, to make sure she wasn't involved."

Linda might have said many things, but being

Linda, she only said the right one: "Call as soon as you can."

I took a cab from La Guardia to the East Side precinct house and told the cop at the desk I wanted to talk to whoever was handling the murder of the Arabs and the three women. He looked me up and down as if maybe I had a bomb in my pocket, then barked into a telephone. A moment later, a short, wiry, balding man in shirt-sleeves appeared. "I'm Sergeant DeMarco," he said.

"My name's Malloy. I may have information about those murders on the East Side."

He led me down a corridor to a small, windowless office. He settled behind the desk, nodded me into the chair opposite, and said, "Let's have it."

"A few days ago I was in New York on business and—"

"What business?"

"I'm a writer. I was staying at the Algonquin, and one evening I was having a drink there when a young woman came in and we started talking. She was about twenty, tall, blonde, nice-looking. She said her name was Blair. We—"

"First name or last?"

"First. She never told me her last name. I asked her to have dinner with me. She said that first she needed to go uptown and see a friend. We took a cab to a new apartment building on First near Eighty-third. We went up to 33-B. Her friend was a blonde named Monica. There were three other young women there and four Arab men."

"Names?"

"I never knew them; we only stayed a few minutes. But when I saw the story in today's *Times* I thought it must be the same apartment and some of the same people. I was afraid one of the dead women might be Blair, so I came up to see if I could help with the identification."

DeMarco had a bony, lopsided, unpleasant face. He stared at me for a long time, gnawing on a toothpick. I started to feel uneasy, even though I didn't see how he could punch many holes in my story. It was mostly true, except for the key fact that I knew exactly who Blair was.

"Where is it you live, Mr. Malloy?"

"In Virginia. Near Washington, D.C."

"ID?"

I tossed my driver's license across the desk. He scowled at it a moment, then said, "And you flew up here this morning because you were worried about a girl you'd only met once? To identify a girl whose last name you don't know?"

DeMarco's ugly face was reddening; he looked as if he were about to slap the cuffs on me. Did he think I was the nutty criminal who returned to the scene of the crime?

"That's right."

"What happened after you left the apartment? Did you take the girl to dinner?"

"Yes." I told him where.

"Did you have sex with this . . . Blair?"

"No, dammit, I didn't. Look, do you want me to identify the dead people or not?"

DeMarco's little eyes glittered. "Sure," he said, and tossed a manila envelope across the desk.

I was relieved as I pulled out the photographs. Until that moment I thought I'd be looking at corpses in the morgue. Thank God I didn't; the pictures were bad enough.

I recognized the young Arab, Ahmad; even in death he looked scornful.

I recognized Monica, her green eyes closed forever.

But the three other men and two other women were unknown to me.

"That's all of them?" I asked.

"Isn't it enough?"

"Monica I recognize. The others I don't know."

I was ready to go now that I knew Bonnie wasn't among the victims, but DeMarco had questions. I gave him more details, that I'd seen one of the Arabs packing a gun, that I'd seen cocaine used, and when I was tired of answering questions, I asked one: What did he think had happened?

He made a chilly shrug. "It could have been a

robbery. The Wilcox woman was running a cathouse and kept cash and drugs around. The Arabs probably had big bucks in their pockets. So somebody robs 'em and leaves no witnesses."

I shook my head. I didn't think this was a routine robbery, and I couldn't believe he thought so.

DeMarco stood up. "How much longer are you in town, Mr. Malloy?"

Until he asked the question I hadn't thought of it, but now I realized I couldn't leave yet. "Until tomorrow, I guess."

"Staying where?"

"The Algonquin."

DeMarco's smile was truly nasty. "Yeah, you have a lot of luck there, don't you?"

I had to find Bonnie and get her out of New York.

But where was she? I tried to come up with leads, and the only ones I could think of were Buzz, the kid at the apartment house, and Annette, the knockout in the "So Many Men" T-shirt who'd been Bonnie's roommate for a while.

After I checked into my hotel, I did return to the scene of the crime, literally. Buzz was still behind the desk, playing solitaire. At the rear of the lobby, a man in an easy chair was hidden behind a newspaper.

"Remember me, Buzz?" I kept my voice low.

His face was a sullen, pocked mask. "Nah."

"I was here with Bon . . . with Blair a couple of weeks ago. I'm looking for her."

"Bug off, man."

"Help me find her and I'll make it worth your while."

"You deaf, man? Haul ass. You want I should call the cops?"

"What's your problem?" I demanded. "I thought you were her friend."

He sprang out of the chair and started pushing me toward the door. I gave ground, fearing a knife. "Why won't you talk?" I asked.

"Back off, asshole!"

We were out the door, and he was still cursing. Then, under his breath, he said, "Toby's, the bar around the corner, meet me at midnight."

With that, he pushed me sprawling to the sidewalk and danced back inside. I picked myself up slowly, glanced in once, wondering who the man behind the newspaper was, then limped away.

Next stop, the Village. Washington Square was packed with pigeons, bums, lousy guitarists, and world-class Frisbee throwers. I spent the evening asking bartenders if they knew a big, good-looking girl named Annette. I got a lot of funny looks and a few leads; with any encouragement, I left my phone number and the promise of a reward.

At midnight I was back uptown, in a booth at

Toby's, a decent little bar with jazz on the jukebox, waiting for Buzz. I waited an hour, drank two beers, blew a buck on early Sinatra, then left, convinced the kid had been jerking me around.

I had stepped to the curb, looking for a cab, when someone said, "Over here."

Buzz was lurking in an alley, almost invisible among the shadows. I didn't like joining him there; entering dark alleys with sullen strangers is not my idea of smart. But I'd come too far to argue.

"I was inside."

"Shut up and listen. Your girlfriend came down the freight elevator, and I let her out the back door."

It took me a moment to catch up. "Where is she now?"

"How the hell do I know? If I was her, I'd be in fucking Nebraska, my ass still in high gear."

I was still a half step behind. "Are you saying she was there the night of the murders?"

"You got shit for brains, man? What are we talking about?"

"Who did it, Buzz? Who are they?"

"Look, I like the chick, so I'm telling you she got lucky. And that's it."

"I can pay you."

I heard a snort of laughter. "Not like them other guys you can't."

As if on cue, a limousine cruised slowly by. I froze

in the shadows until it passed. When I turned around, Buzz was gone.

I was awakened the next morning by DeMarco banging on my door. He had a big, potato-faced Irish cop with him, Gohegan by name. I sent for coffee and juice, then faced them. "You could have called first."

"We were in the neighborhood," DeMarco said with his sweet little smile. "We've got questions."

"Ask."

"You said you took the girl to dinner. You didn't say you brought her back here afterward."

I shrugged. So the boys had been doing some checking. "We sat in the lobby and talked for a while."

"Then you took her up to your room."

"Okay. We were talking, and they closed the lobby."

"You still say you didn't have sex with her?"

"Dammit, DeMarco, are you investigating seven murders or my goddamn sex life? Number one, no I didn't; number two, what difference would it make?"

"We'll ask the questions. What did you two talk about for three hours?"

"I told you, I'm a writer. I wanted to hear her story, and she felt like talking."

"And in three hours you didn't get her address or full name or phone number? Or the names of any of her customers?"

I muttered something about her not wanting to mention names. By now I looked like a damn fool, but all I could do was stick to my story.

The Irishman stopped scowling long enough to ask, "At the Wilcox woman's apartment, did anyone else come by? Or call? Or get mentioned?"

I suddenly thought of Nicky Allegro, the burly, evil-eyed pusher. I would have loved to turn the cops loose on that bastard, but he knew too much about Bonnie.

I slowly shook my head. "Nothing I can think of."

It's no fun being a lousy liar; I was sure they could read me like a billboard.

"One other thing," Gohegan said. "Where were you the night of the murders?"

"At home. With my wife."

DeMarco stood up. "You ought to stay there."

After they left, a bartender called and said he knew where Annette was. I took a cab downtown and traded fifty dollars for an address, then met briefly with a girl named Annette who looked nothing at all like the one I was seeking.

At that point I gave up. I was tired and frustrated and increasingly aware that I was in trouble. I was telling the cops a crazy, half-assed story that could blow up in my face, and I was spinning my wheels in my search for Bonnie. All I could do was go home and hope she called me.

I was back at the Algonquin, about to check out, when I decided to call Penny; at least I could reassure her that Bonnie wasn't dead.

She has her own phone in her dormitory room, a luxury unknown in my college days. And she answered it; Penny seems to attend classes rarely, if at all.

"Listen, sweetheart, I'm in New York. I didn't find Bonnie, but I found out she wasn't one of the people killed. But she's still in trouble. If she calls you, tell her to call me as soon as she can."

"Tell her yourself," my daughter said brightly. "She's right here."

7

I clutched the phone and tried not to cry out in rage.

"What do you *mean* she's right there?"

"I picked her up at the bus station an hour ago. Daddy, she had to go *somewhere*. She thinks these *gangsters* are looking for her in New York."

My blood ran cold. It might be a joke to Penny, but I'd seen the pictures of those women with their brains blown out. "I'll be there as soon as I can. Don't let her go anywhere or call anybody. Just sit tight. Do you understand?"

"Of course, Daddy."

I made the noon shuttle, then got around to the *Times*, where a new surprise lurked.

Khalid Yassin, identified in the first story as a businessman, was now described as "a senior official of Saudi intelligence." The two other men, in their forties, were listed as "security agents," and the boy Ahmad was said to be Khalid's nephew.

This thing kept getting worse. I didn't know much

about the Middle East, but I knew that when a top Saudi spook got himself killed in a New York cathouse, the sauce was likely to hit the fan. All I wanted was to get Bonnie out of the line of fire.

It wasn't just the call-girl episode anymore. She might have information about some very ugly murders, the kind that tended to inspire more murders. I went over it again and again, and it always came out the same: I had to take Bonnie to her father, and she had to tell him the truth. Then Harry and his lawyer could deal with the New York police. Maybe the call-girl connection could be quietly forgotten; nobody was mad at Bonnie. But no matter what happened, we had to come clean. It was a classic example of an old political maxim: When all else fails, tell the truth.

I picked up my car at the Washington airport and drove straight to Charlottesville; in all, my trip took five hours, from the Algonquin to Penny's ivy-covered dorm. It was a crisp, clear fall afternoon. I thought I'd take the girls to dinner, then have a private talk with Bonnie to persuade her to level with her father. My guess was that she was ready to have it out with her parents, ready to inflict and suffer whatever pain was necessary before the healing could begin.

As I walked toward the dorm, I realized something was wrong. I saw faces in the windows, sensed the eerie silence that filled the quadrangle instead of the usual bedlam of rock flowing from every room.

A young cop, posted outside the dorm, asked my business. There'd never been a cop there before. I told him my daughter was inside and showed my ID. "It's the Malloy girl's father," he called to the sergeant in the lobby.

My knees grew weak, and I wasn't sure I could speak. I'd been a police reporter, known grim after-the-tragedy silences like this. But what could have happened in the five hours since I'd talked to Penny?

Penny's roommate burst through the door and embraced me. "Oh, God, Mr. Malloy."

"What is it, Meredith?"

She took my arm and led me toward their room. Young faces, unnaturally pale and solemn, peered out of doorways. We entered the room—Penny's un-changing shambles of books, records, clothes, empty bottles, and cigarette packs, and atop one mountain of debris, the teddy bear I gave her for her fifth birth-day. My tough-talking, beer-swigging daughter rarely sleeps without her Teddy.

I looked at Meredith, an elegant girl, mature be-yond her years; now her hands trembled. "Where is she?"

"In the infirmary. These men, they broke in here, looking for Bonnie. They . . . they hit Penny."

"Where's Bonnie?"

"I don't know."

"What about the men?"

"Come on, I'll take you to the infirmary."
I picked up the teddy bear and followed her.

Penny was sitting up in bed, giving a nurse a hard time about something. She hugged me and Teddy and cried a little. She had a shiner and a sore jaw, but Penny is a hard one to silence. As soon as Meredith and the nurse left, I pulled my chair close to the bed and took her hand. "Okay, baby, what happened?"

She was propped up on some pillows, her long dirty-blonde hair fanned out around her, an angel with a black eye. "These two guys walked into the dorm—you know how people just come and go. They knocked on the door and said, 'Penny?' I said, 'Come in, it's open,' and there they were, one of them with a gun. Before I could even yell, he grabbed me and said, 'Where is she?' I said, 'Who?' and he knocked hell out of me. I mean, this guy was not taking any crap. The other one grabbed Meredith, maybe thought she was Bonnie, and the first one hit me again—I guess I kicked him—and God knows what might have happened, except the door opened and there was Bonnie. She'd gone out for cigarettes.

"I don't know if she knew the guys, but she got the message. I mean, she started running, and they started after her, except I tripped the one who'd been hitting me. I think Bonnie got away."

"You *think* she did?"

"On the landing, halfway down the stairs, the window was open. I think she jumped. It's ten feet to the ground; then she could have followed the trees to the next dorm. A Phi Delt's BMW is missing from there."

"The men got away?"

"Gone like a cool breeze."

"What'd they look like?"

Penny made a face. "It happened so fast. And they wore hats. Young guys. Dark-skinned. One had a scar on the end of his nose. Maybe Mexicans or something."

"Why Mexican?"

"When one of them spoke to the other one, it sounded like Spanish. The thing is, we were really lucky. If Bonnie had been here when they came, they'd have gotten what they came for."

"What do you mean? Gotten what? Bonnie?"

"No, no, the tape. She had it in her pocket."

"What tape? Slow down. What are you talking about?"

Penny reached for the water pitcher and tossed down two aspirin. "The cassette the Arab gave Bonnie the night everybody was killed." She sighed. "God, Daddy, you don't know anything, do you?"

This is what Bonnie told Penny about the murders:

The idea was that Ahmad, the young Arab prince, was giving a surprise party for his uncle Khalid, who had arrived in New York that morning. Four or five Arabs were expected, and Monica wanted her top-of-the-line girls there to entertain them. Ahmad had said that if his uncle liked the girls, he might fly some of them to Palm Beach after he finished his business in New York and Washington.

That was the plan, but it wasn't going well when Bonnie arrived at nine. Some of the girls hadn't shown up, and the other Arabs had for unknown reasons been delayed. Moreover, Khalid was nervous and preoccupied, despite Monica's efforts to charm him. His bodyguards sat like lumps. Two other girls were there, but no one would talk to them.

Finally, Monica got some champagne down Khalid and jollied him into taking a tour of the apartment. He brightened a little and invited Bonnie and Ahmad to come along. They ascended the spiral staircase and checked out the Jacuzzi and the game room and finally settled on Monica's big, round revolving bed.

Khalid loved that bed. He was said to own castles in Spain, villas in Switzerland, mansions in Beverly Hills, apartment buildings on Park Avenue, and seventy-seven Rolls-Royces, but he had never seen a revolving bed before. They sat there, talking and drinking ("spinning and sinning," as Monica put it), and he started to relax. "It is very difficult," he said. "I am in your country on most serious business." Still, he was showing signs of interest in Monica when the doorbell rang.

"It's the caterers," Monica said. She jumped up, but Khalid seized her wrist. "Ahmad can see to it," he said, and his nephew dutifully marched downstairs.

Khalid and Monica started to get cozy, and Bonnie offered to leave, but he said, "No, stay," and she guessed he had designs on them both; such things were not unknown in Monica's revolving bed. Then they heard a cry downstairs.

Khalid ran to the door, then slammed it shut, pale as death. "What is it?" Monica demanded.

"My enemies," he said.

Monica started out to confront the intruders— nobody was going to break up *her* party—and Khalid turned to Bonnie. He took a tape cassette from his pocket and said, "Hide this. Hide yourself. Take it to my embassy and they will pay you."

They heard footsteps in the hall. Khalid tried to barricade the door, and Bonnie ran into Monica's dressing room. There was a walk-in closet packed with expensive robes, slippers, and nightgowns. What Bonnie knew, because Monica had once shown her, was that at the back of the closet was a hidden panel that opened into a tiny compartment, hardly bigger than a phone booth. The original idea had been to put a camera there to film the bedroom antics; that hadn't been done, and Monica used the space to store jewels and drugs.

Bonnie slipped through the opening, shut the panel behind her, and sat trembling in the darkness, clutching the cassette. She heard the intruders break into the bedroom and Khalid screaming as they dragged him out. For many minutes there was only terrifying silence; then she heard cries and groans from below. She grew fearful that the intruders would come and find her, and when she heard the first shot, she knew she must flee no matter what the risk.

She crept out of her hiding place, tiptoed down the hallway, let herself out an upstairs door, and took the freight elevator to the basement. The last thing she heard was Khalid's cries for mercy. In the basement, she found the doors locked and, afraid the killers might be watching the lobby, called Buzz to unlock the door to the alley.

She took the subway to the West Side bus terminal and caught the next bus to Washington. En route, she grew afraid, and she got off in Philadelphia and spent the rest of the weekend hiding in a cheap hotel there. Finally, she had the idea of seeking refuge with Penny—what better hideout for an eighteen-year-old girl than a huge university?—and she caught a bus to Charlottesville. Then, somehow, her refuge there proved to be no refuge at all.

"How did they find her, Daddy?" It was past ten, and the nurse had given up on evicting me.

"Someone might have told them you were a friend of hers. Or it could have been phone records. She called you a lot, didn't she? So when they decide she's skipped town, they start checking her friends outside New York."

"Is it that easy to check somebody's phone records?"

"It depends who you are."

"God, you make it sound like the mob or something."

I just looked at her; I had no reassurances to offer.

"Poor Bonnie, she'll never stop running. She'll think she's not safe anywhere."

"She may not be."

"Daddy, who *are* they?"

"I don't know. Khalid was a top-level intelligence officer. A lot of people might want to kill him or to steal his secrets. Did Bonnie take the tape with her?"

"I guess so."

"Penny, did you *listen* to the damn thing?"

"We thought about it. I wanted to, but those guys came before we did."

It had been a long day, and I needed some sleep. "I've got to find a place to stay," I said.

"You're not leaving me here alone," Penny declared. "Let's check me out; then we can both go sleep in my room."

"What about Meredith?"

"She went to stay with her boyfriend— You think she'd stay there alone?"

"Tomorrow, after I leave, I want you and Meredith to change rooms in case those bastards come back."

"Oh Daddy, that'd take forever," my daughter replied. "But maybe we should."

Penny and I returned to her room about midnight. The next morning I was awakened by a girl who wanted to bum a cigarette and was entirely indifferent to the spectacle of a middle-aged man in Meredith's bed. There followed an hour of shouts, giggles, curses, banging doors, flushing toilets, loud music, and whirring hair dryers as the girls departed for classes. Penny, however, never seemed to have classes before afternoon, so we strolled across Mr. Jefferson's noble Lawn to the strip of campus hangouts called the Corner. We claimed the front booth, by the window, at the Virginian, and embarked on a leisurely breakfast of scrambled eggs, country sausage, and beer.

"Did you know Milton Loftis got drunk in here?" she asked me over coffee.

"Who?"

"Milton Loftis. In *Lie Down In Darkness*. There's a scene here, in the Virginian."

"I'd forgotten," I said. The child *is* well-read.

As I was paying the bill, Penny dug in her purse and produced a spiral notebook and a small address book. "Bonnie said to give these to you. One is her date book—you know, like names and addresses. The other one is, I don't know, something she wrote."

I stuck the books in my pocket—I wasn't ready to deal with them yet—and we walked back to my car. I was about to say good-bye when she surprised me again.

"Have you got a few minutes? There's something I'd like to show you."

She drove me to a tree-shaded old mansion on the outskirts of town that proved to be a state-supported orphanage. We were quickly surrounded by a couple of dozen leaping, squealing children, all seeking Penny's attention. She hugged and greeted them and in time introduced me. She made those kids glow; Penny's always been great with children.

In time a stout woman in her sixties joined us. "Your daughter has been such a blessing to us," she whispered, then rushed off to break up a scuffle between two boys. Penny tossed a ball for a while, wiped some runny noses, talked at length with a tearful six-year-old girl, then said her good-byes, crying, "See you tomorrow, guys," as we left. Kids trailed us to the car, demanding a final embrace.

"I've been volunteering there two afternoons a week," she told me as we drove away. "A girl in my dorm took me, and I just had to. Aren't they precious?"

"Why didn't you tell us?"

Penny shrugged and reached for a cigarette. "I was afraid you'd, you know, say that I should be studying."

"Baby, am I that unreasonable?"

"Sometimes."

I sighed. Maybe I was that unreasonable sometimes. Anyway, I was proud of her and told her so. Penny does a lot of things I hate, like smoking and otherwise abusing her body and sometimes being as stubborn and intolerant as I am. (The gods, for our sins, give us children like ourselves.) She also does things that fill me with unspeakable joy. As a better writer than I once warned, anyone seeking a moral in this narrative will be shot.

I arrived home in midafternoon and finally told Linda the truth about Bonnie, the whole damn thing.

Her eyes filled with tears. "We've got to help her."

"I know."

"What are you going to do?"

"Talk to Harry. She's his daughter."

"But what about—?"

"The call-girl bit? No, I won't break that to Harry. Someone else can do that."

"She must want so much to hurt them."

"She found the way. Kids have a knack for that."

"But this . . . this tape—what could be on it?"

I shrugged. "A code? A list of names? Military plans? Something important enough to kill for."

"We should bring Penny home from school."

I'd already thought of that one. "In the first place, she wouldn't come. In the second place, she's probably safer there."

Linda's eyes widened. Maybe I shouldn't have hit her with that one. But I'd been thinking about those notebooks of Bonnie's I had. I'd glanced at them on the way home. They were written in a semicode but seemed to list some of her customers and to describe some of their bizarre sexual tastes. Maybe the killers would think I had the tape, too, and come looking for it. Our home is not the most secure place in America; we never even lock our doors.

Linda poured herself a shot of bourbon, neat, tossed it down, then went out to her garden and started resolutely digging for a few last potatoes.

I thought things over for a while, then called Harry Prescott and said I needed to talk to him about Bonnie. He told me to come at once.

The great tidal wave of rush-hour traffic was pouring out of Washington as I drove in; I arrived at the Senate just after six. I parked in one of the By Permit Only zones; they don't check them in the evenings. Harry had one of those big, charmless offices in the Hart Building. His staff played basketball in there when he was away. Literally. It was not a reassuring sight to see the key advisers to a potential president leaping around his office playing basketball. Those clowns could be running America soon.

I didn't have a Senate ID, so I went through the public entrance, hurried into the big echoing lobby, beneath the huge mobile *Mountains and Clouds*, or whatever it's called, and took the elevator up to Harry's office. Entering, I was unnerved to confront Orth Butler, Harry's father-in-law.

Orth was a craggy white-haired man in his seventies who'd made a lot of money during the war and dabbled in politics ever since. He gave big bucks to both parties, and as a result, the White House door was almost always open to him. His connections had enabled him to pull off some pioneering import deals with the Russians, and for more than thirty years he'd maintained a sort of one-man foreign policy. He'd cultivated three generations of Soviet leaders, and when things got tight, several American presidents had sent him on missions to Moscow.

I met Orth soon after Harry and I became neighbors. He went out of his way to cultivate me, probably because he knew I moonlighted as a speech writer for several senators. After my first novel bombed, when I was seriously broke, Orth took me to lunch at the Cosmos Club, sought my advice on various affairs of state, and asked if I could use a loan "until things pick up." I thought he was trying to buy into my political connections and politely declined. Things were never quite the same after that. We were cordial, but there was an edge. Turning down a rich man's money is like turning down a beautiful woman's body; they never quite forgive you.

Not that I disliked Orth; I didn't. Over the years he'd done things I admired, like telling Lyndon Johnson he was insane to pursue a war in Vietnam. Still, it was unsettling to find him there, because Orth is a far more devious man than his son-in-law and thus was far more likely to sense that I was not telling the whole truth about Bonnie. To give Harry his due, that might have been why he summoned the old man.

Harry greeted me gravely. "What's this about Bonnie?"

I told them the highlights: Bonnie's call to Penny, my meeting with Bonnie in New York, our visit to Monica's apartment. When Harry tried to interrupt, Orth Butler snapped, "Let him finish!"

All I left out was the call-girl connection. The New York police could fill in that little detail. I said Bonnie had wanted to reconcile with her parents and asked my advice.

Finally, I got to the murders—the "Penthouse Massacre," the tabloids were calling it. They gasped when I told them Bonnie had been present the night of the killings and barely escaped with her life. Grimly, I wound up my story: the mysterious tape, Bonnie's flight to Charlottesville, the attack there and her flight.

"That's the story," I concluded. "I'm sorry."

"Sorry!" Harry yelled. "Why the hell didn't you tell me about this sooner?"

Ah, yes, Senator, blame the messenger who brings the bad news; I'd expected that.

"There wasn't much to tell, until—" I began, but Orth cut me off.

"Harry, keep a civil tongue in your head; this man is trying to help us."

Harry nodded slowly. "Sorry, Grady. You can understand what a shock this is."

"Of course."

"Tell me, did these people . . . did they know Bonnie was my daughter?"

"I'm almost sure they didn't. She called herself Blair up there, and nobody seemed to use last names."

"Her full name is Elizabeth Blair Prescott, of course," Orth said.

Harry looked unpersuaded. "It could be a plot to get me," he mused aloud. "To set me up somehow."

Such paranoia is not unknown in his profession, or always unwarranted. "I don't think so, Harry," I said. "I think she was just a pretty girl who got involved with the wrong people."

"How *did* she meet this . . . this Monica?" he demanded.

"My impression is that Monica was someone

who gave a lot of parties and knew a lot of people. To someone Bonnie's age, she would have seemed glamorous."

I was trying to make it easy for him. But I thought I saw a certain knowing gleam in Orth's eyes. He had been a widower in New York for fifteen years, and I suspected he'd enjoyed a few Monicas in his time. But not Harry. Harry would meet Monica at a party and talk about the deficit.

"Were drugs being used there?" Harry asked. The Senate had discovered cocaine that year and declared it a greater threat to American well-being than poverty, the arms race, and the national debt combined.

"The Arabs had some cocaine," I said. "I didn't see Bonnie use any."

"She's never used drugs," he assured us. "But, dammit, you never know. These pushers use drugs to lure girls into trouble."

"The issue is to locate Bonnie," Orth said impatiently. "And to identify the killers, since they may think Bonnie has Khalid Yassin's tape."

I noted how easily the name rolled off his tongue. "Do you know him?" I asked. "Khalid Yassin, I mean."

"He was quite a well-known man," Orth said dryly, as if amused by my ignorance.

"Did Palmach kill him?" Harry said abruptly.

"How in the world would I know?" the older man shot back. "Let's make our plans— How do we find Bonnie? I take it you don't know where she is, Grady?"

"No." As soon as I said it, the things I didn't have to say, shouldn't have said, just popped out. "But I have some ideas. I asked Penny where she thought Bonnie would go. She thinks she'll go back to New York, try to lose herself there. Maybe she'll call—call Penny or me or you—but if I went to New York and knocked on enough doors, I might be able to find her."

"Then go to New York immediately," Orth said. "Stay in my suite at the Waldorf. Money is no object. Just find the child. And that damned tape, too."

"Wait a minute." I was starting to have second thoughts. "They raided my daughter's dormitory room; my house might be next. I can't go off and leave Linda alone."

"Maybe your wife would like a vacation," Orth said. I noted how he had taken charge. "My plane could fly her down to my villa at Little Dix Bay. I promise you she'll be secure there. Two presidents have vacationed there."

"I'll ask her."

"He should talk to Lee Draper," Harry said.

"Yes, I was just thinking that," Orth agreed. "I have a man in New York who can work with you."

"Who is he?" I asked.

Harry handed me a card that said "Lee Draper, Security Consultant" and gave a 212 phone number.

"Lee was a Senate investigator," Harry said. "I'll call him. When can you get started?"

My doubts were returning, but it seemed too late to turn back. "In the morning, I guess."

They nodded approvingly.

Would the lovely Linda care to be flown by private plane for a free vacation in a pink-walled villa high above Little Dix Bay?

No, no, a thousand times no. The damsel would die before yielding to such a fate!

"These . . . these *thugs* aren't going to run me out of my home!" was how she put it.

"A week in the lap of luxury. Orchids. Rum. Servants. Starry nights. Moonlight rippling on the water."

"No one to scratch my back."

"All right, I'll stay here with you."

"No, you've got to find Bonnie. Harry Prescott and that awful Orth Butler won't do anything right. You go ahead. I'll be fine."

I dug out my gun. Many years ago thieves broke into our first apartment and stole my stereo and Linda's jewelry. Like any red-blooded American boy, I went berserk. I rushed out, vowing revenge, and bought a Saturday night special—my six-shooter, Linda called it. I had a vague plan to lure the intruders into returning, whereupon I'd gun them down. Instead, I regained my senses and hid the revolver in an old sneaker deep in my closet. I hadn't thought of it in years, except once, when I considered murdering a book reviewer.

It is, of course, insane to keep a handgun in your home. Why? Because it is a scientific fact that somewhere in America, every thirty-seven minutes, a woman picks up a handgun and shoots a man; in 78.9 percent of the cases the man is her husband, in 83.5 percent the woman has never before fired a gun, and in 96.7 percent she puts the first shot right between his eyes.

In other words, a man who keeps a gun around the house has only himself to blame when they come to carry him away.

Nonetheless, I had one, and I dug it out, cleaned it up, and offered it to Linda for protection while I was in New York. "Put that awful thing away!" she cried, as if to a flasher.

So I returned to New York and took my six-shooter with me, checked in my bag.

On the flight up, I tried to remember all the names Bonnie had mentioned, and I took a closer look at the date book she'd given Penny. It was mostly written with initials and abbreviations, but there were some phone numbers, and I thought I could track down at least some of her customers.

The other notebook was something else entirely. Apparently, after we talked, Bonnie began to set down the details of some of her sexual adventures as raw material for our proposed book. I read a little and then didn't want to read any more. The one that stopped me was a stockbroker who would dress Bonnie in his daughter's confirmation dress, throw her down on the kitchen floor, screaming, "You bitch! You slut!" and act out a rape of her, then later tearfully beg her forgiveness.

Orth Butler's apartment in the Waldorf Towers was all that I'd expected—three bedrooms, Persian rugs, a mix of Impressionist and pre-Columbian art, fresh flowers in the vases. One wall featured photographs of him deep-sea fishing with Hemingway, boozing with Khrushchev, golfing with Nixon, and dancing with Ava Gardner. The man had led quite a life. A call from downstairs informed me that a car and driver awaited my pleasure. That meant Orth would know every place I went, but did it matter? We were on the same side, weren't we?

Bonnie had mentioned a woman named Ruth who worked in real estate and booked girls on the side. I got out the yellow pages and started calling and acting dumb until a woman said, "Oh, you must mean Ruth *Orlando*—she's at Hedrick and Waller."

I had my surly young chauffeur drive me up Park to the real estate office, where I asked for Ruth Orlando. About that time a rather spectacular blonde, mid-fortyish, breezed past, all cheekbones and eyelashes and gold bracelets. "Ms. Orlando, a gentleman to see you," the receptionist said.

The blonde shot me a quizzical glance. "Yes?" Her lips were the color of blood and her eyes the color of money.

I told her my name but not my business. She gave me a brittle smile and said she was late for an appointment.

"I have a car and driver outside," I announced grandly. "Perhaps I could drop you."

I thought she was the type to be impressed by Orth's limo, and I was right. Soon we were settled in its sweet, warm womb, and she was asking, "Now, Mr. Malloy, tell me what you're looking for. A nice condo? Or a brownstone, perhaps?"

"Actually I'm looking for two young women. Blair and Annette are their names."

Ruth Orlando showed no distress at having her second career thus introduced; rather, she seemed amused. "Oh, *those* two— How in the world did you link me with them?"

"I met them in the Village last week. I said I was house hunting, and they mentioned you as a friend in the real estate business. I lost their phone numbers but remembered your name."

"Aren't you clever? Well, I'll *try* to help you, but you know how these young girls move around."

"I was hoping to see them tonight."

"Both of them?"

"If possible."

"Goodness. Let me make a suggestion. Drop by my apartment—tennish. Some people will be there. Perhaps Blair and Annette. If not, some other interesting young women. Do I take it you prefer *young* women?"

I gave her a raffish smile. "I am a man who values experience."

We reached her stop, and she handed me her card. "Don't misunderstand," I said. "I want to talk to those girls, and I'll pay you for your trouble."

Ruth Orlando took her card back and wrote something on the back of it. "Blair changes apartments more or less weekly. I'll give you Annette's address." I glanced at the address and handed her two hundred-dollar bills; she was clearly a woman who liked cash on the barrelhead.

"Thank you," she said after a glance at the bills. "Do drop by tonight. I'm sure we have a lot in common."

I went straight to the address she had given me, a new apartment building in the Village, near the corner of Bleecker and Thompson. It may have been Annette's apartment, but no one was home, and the doorman wasn't answering any questions. I was back on the sidewalk, wondering what to do next, when a man approached me.

"Grady Malloy?"

He was about forty, tall and lean, with a guarded, handsome face and close-cropped salt-and-pepper hair, but what I noticed most was his clothing. The penny loafers, the pleatless charcoal flannels, the blue-and-white striped button-down shirt, the cream-colored foulard tie with the maroon design, the exquisite gray tweed coat—not one American man in a thousand has the audacity to mix those ingredients and know he'll come out right. You can't learn to dress like that in college; college is too late. To dress like that, somebody has to start you very young so that by twelve you're a proper little preppy who understands that a wise man buys his shirts at Brooks Brothers but never his suits. This fellow's outfit proclaimed his membership in an American elite, one I associated with inherited wealth, the oldest law firms, certain Tory elements at the CIA, and such great Americans as George Bush and Pierre (Pete) du Pont.

I kept staring at the man until he said, "Grady? I'm Lee Draper. Have you had lunch?"

I admitted I had not.

"There's a neat little deli around the corner."

I sighed (it is unforgivable for a grown man to call a deli "neat") and let him lead me there. It was a fine old neighborhood. The Circle In The Square was nearby, and the theater where Linda and I had seen *The Fantastiks*, years before. T-shirt emporia and pottery shops were mixed in with family-style Greek and Italian restaurants that had been there forever. I wondered how Draper had found me. Probably the driver was reporting on my whereabouts. There is no such thing as a free limo.

The deli was the real thing. Draper ordered hot pastrami on rye with mustard and a beer. I asked for the same, and we took a table by the window, where I could see my limo idling in a No Parking zone.

"Harry gave me your card," I said. "I was planning to call."

Lee Draper cocked an eyebrow. He looked intelligent as well as elegant, but there was something hard and arrogant about his face—the glint of the eyes, the twist of the mouth. I believe in faces the way the FBI believes in fingerprints—I think they tell you most of what you need to know about people—and Draper's left me cold.

"Frankly, Orth is worried about you," he said.

I had my doubts about that. "Exactly what do you do?"

His smile was razor-sharp. "I keep people alive."

"Business must be good."

"Smashing."

Again he had managed to offend me. I'm in the word business, and I've developed a lot of perhaps irrational prejudices. I loathe people who use the word "smashing." Not to mention the expression "early on," the phrase "a wide variety," and such psuedo-words as "pricey" and "smarmy."

"And I'm to receive your protection?"

"Orth greatly appreciates your willingness to search for the girl. But there may be some very dangerous people involved in this affair, and he doesn't want you to risk harm in what is not ultimately your concern."

It was a pretty speech, and I didn't believe a word of it. Remember, I'm an expert on pretty speeches.

"Yesterday he was anxious that I come here," I said.

"He's reconsidered."

"Therefore he suggests I catch the next plane home?"

Draper raised his hands magnanimously. "Therefore you could stay and relax at the Waldorf for a few days. Or let us fly you and your wife down to Little Dix. But first give me whatever leads you have and I'll pursue them."

The more generous this fellow became, the more pissed off was I. Orth Butler was jerking me around. Yesterday he wanted my help. Today he sends Mr. Smooth to dismiss me.

And there was this: My leads involved Bonnie's fling as a call girl, and I wasn't ready to reveal that to this fellow or to Orth Butler.

And finally this: When Bonnie was in trouble, she hadn't gone to Daddy Warbucks for help, she'd come to me, and she might have had her reasons. Part of me loved that girl and hated what her rich, powerful, screwed-up family had done to her. I wasn't ready to surrender her fate to them, not yet.

I sipped my beer. "I've already made a few calls. I'll finish what I'm doing; then, if I have anything, I'll turn it over to you."

Draper patted his lips with a paper napkin. Three vertical lines appeared on his forehead, as if I had put him under severe strain. The more I looked at him, the more I thought he looked like a very worried man. I wondered if it was just I who had him worried or if he had bigger problems. "Grady, I think I should tell you that Orth and I are aware of . . . of Bonnie's *association* with Monica Wilcox."

"Does Harry know?"

"No. When Orth learned of it, his instinct, like your own, was to extricate the girl from the situation without causing her parents needless heartbreak."

More pretty words. "What did he do?"

"He spoke to me. I said I would speak to Monica, then to Bonnie if necessary, in the role of family friend. But before I could act, the Arabs were killed and the situation became far more complicated."

I still didn't like him, but at least we were getting somewhere. "I assume Orth told you about the tape and about the two thugs who followed Bonnie to Charlottesville."

Draper brushed a few imaginary crumbs off his

right sleeve. "Grady, the situation calls for extreme realism."

I thought I might hit the son of a bitch if he called me Grady once more.

"I can't prove it," he continued, "but those murders look to me like a Palmach operation."

I asked him what Palmach was.

Draper glanced around the quiet little deli and lowered his voice, although no one was within ten feet of us.

"Palmach is a semiautonomous offshoot of Mossad, the Israeli secret service. They have a very flexible, very secret offensive force operating in the U.S., with unlimited funds at its disposal. In effect, they are an extremely potent guerrilla army protecting Israeli interests."

"A hit squad?"

Draper shrugged. "That's rhetoric. They do tend to react to PLO outrages, here and abroad. Watch the papers closely and you'll notice the unexplained deaths of certain Arab leaders from time to time. The point is that these are extremely lethal individuals, and we don't want them pursuing Bonnie—or you or me, for that matter."

"Why would they kill all those people? What could be on that damn cassette?"

"I don't know what's on it. As for killing people, that's their line of work."

"Young women?"

"That's unusual, and perhaps reflects the gravity of the matter. Of course, I could be wrong; it might not have been Palmach. All I know for certain is that two members of the Saudi royal family have been assassinated and the Saudis won't take it lying down. They'll strike back; my job is to keep Bonnie from getting caught in the crossfire. I wish you'd make my job easier by cooperating."

Am I stubborn? Thickheaded? Irrational? A damned fool sometimes? Yes, yes, yes.

"Let's talk tomorrow," I said. "I've got a few more people to see."

"That is not wise."

"No, it probably isn't," I agreed. "Look, what do you propose?"

He hesitated a moment, as if to impress me with how candid he was about to be. "To pass word to Palmach to lay off Bonnie, that as soon as we find her, we'll give them the tape on a silver platter."

More pretty words with a hollow rattle. Did Orth Butler give anything to anyone on a silver platter?

Why did I dislike Draper so much? It wasn't just him; it was what he represented. You have to understand that modern Washington is awash with money—money and fear and greed. Politicians, desperate to be elected, shake down special-interest groups, desperate for influence. But once the politicians get the money, they don't know what to do with it. Enter the "consultants," a shadowy army of self-anointed experts who for a price will write your speeches, polish your image, create your TV spots, slander your opponent—will perform endless dubious services that have nothing to do with the public interest and everything to do with raping our political system. These mercenaries flock to Washington like flies to shit, and Lee Draper was just one more of them, although better groomed than most.

He followed me out to the street. "I'll be in touch," I said.

My slack-jawed driver shoved open the limo door without getting out. I looked back at Lee Draper, the world's best-dressed specialist in keeping people alive, as he glared at me in disgust.

"Say, were you at Choate?" I asked.

His unhappy face eased into a cautious smile. "Why yes. Were you?"

"No," I said. "I wasn't even close."

10

Bonnie's date book had references to a "G.K." and to "Giles." Her notebook contained this fragment:

G is so pitiful. His wife left him and he hates his job and says everybody is against him. How can he be so famous and powerful and still so unhappy? Sex doesn't make him happy, either. He won't even try. All he wants is for me to tie him to the bedpost with neckties and take off my clothes except for black boots and panties and call him dirty names and whip him. He has a real whip but I wouldn't use it and he begged and finally I whacked him with a belt a few times and he started crying about his mother. It was so sick that I walked out, didn't want the money, but he called me the next day and said how I'd "purified" him and he'd pay me $500 to come back again. Worth it?

I checked the phone numbers, and sure enough, G.K. was none other than Giles Kessler. For a moment I was surprised, but not all that surprised. I'd been hearing stories of Giles's bizarre behavior for years; it was the kind of gossip that reporters exchange over drinks to console themselves that all editors truly are mad.

Giles Kessler is one of the two or three most powerful editors in America. I don't mean the power to close a Broadway show; I mean the power to influence how Americans think and see themselves and who we elect as president. I've known a few such editors in my time, and for all their seeming differences—this one a bookish recluse, that one an alcoholic extrovert—they all want power the way a shark wants your leg. Maybe they started out as happy-go-lucky reporters, but somewhere along the way they changed, glimpsed the Big Picture, until reporters became merely means to an end. To make an omelet, you break eggs; to be a great editor, you break reporters.

The gossip wasn't just that Giles had fired this reporter or demoted that one but that he had set out to destroy some of his in-house critics, until two had breakdowns and another killed himself. But what reporters said didn't matter. Profits were sky-high, and the board of directors thought Giles hung the moon.

I should add that my own occasional dealings

with Giles had always been pleasant. He was a charmer if you didn't work for him.

In Giles's outer office I encountered a stubby, choleric Irishman who told me that Mr. Kessler saw no one without an appointment. When I persisted, he yelled, "Get out or I'll call security!"

I scribbled a note that said, "Giles, I'm looking for Blair. Urgent, Grady Malloy."

"Give him this," I said, but by then the security man had arrived. Fortunately, he proved to be a scrawny rent-a-cop who was decidedly nonviolent. The Irishman was cursing us both, but I was as mad as he was. "Just give him the note, fuckhead," I yelled. That proved to be the sort of talk he understood. He returned in a few minutes to mutter darkly that Mr. Kessler *might* see me later.

Giles let me cool my heels for an hour, but just as I was about to walk out—he was a master of such things—he came charging out to greet me with a two-handed handshake and a barracuda smile. He led me into his vast office—fifty reporters, just down the hall, were crowded into roughly the same space—and poured us both double scotches. Then he settled himself behind a wraparound desk that had three TV monitors atop it and more telephones than the president. I perched across from him in a rickety chair that faced uphill to the throne. It was crude but probably effective.

97

Giles sipped his J&B contentedly. "Now, Grady, who is this Blair? Am I supposed to know him?"

"It's a she, Giles. She's eighteen, tall, blonde, gorgeous, and for the past few months a call girl. Except now she's missing and I'm trying to find her."

"Have you tried the police?"

"Your name and number were in her datebook."

"My name and number could be anywhere."

"Look, I don't enjoy being here, but I think the girl is in danger. Do you have any idea where she might be?"

Giles's face puffed up until he looked as if he might explode. "We've treated you pretty well, haven't we?"

I didn't know what he was talking about.

"Your last book, we called it 'first-rate,' right?"

"True."

"We don't have to be so nice. We've destroyed bigger men than you." He was red-faced, bug-eyed, raving.

"Look, I mean you no harm. I'm just looking for—"

"You're working for Harry Prescott, aren't you?"

So he'd been on the phone to his Washington bureau while I was cooling my heels. "Harry is an old friend, but this has nothing to do with him."

"If Prescott wants to take me on, I'll handle him, too. Senators come and go. You think you can push your way into my office with your cheap blackmail and—"

I stood up. "You're out of your mind. I'm trying to find a missing girl."

He stood and faced me across the desk. His eyes had narrowed to slits. "I know the lies they spread about me," he said. "Filth, gossip, slander. But it doesn't matter; it can't detract from the monument I've created here." His arm swept around the room, its walls crowded with prizes and certificates and pictures of Giles with presidents and kings.

I turned to go. "Forget it," I said. "I'm sorry I asked."

He shot across the room and suddenly was blocking my path. For a moment I thought he was going to attack me. But he was undergoing some sort of transformation, like the Wolf Man when the full moon came out, and gradually a sickly smile spread across his bloated face. I watched in fascination as he brought himself under control, then reached out to take my arm. "Don't leave, Grady," he implored. "I know you're my friend. But you don't know the threats I receive, the enemies I've made, because I fight for the truth."

First I couldn't get in; now I couldn't get out. He poured another drink, then steered us to a sofa where he plopped down beside me, knee to knee. "I felt sorry for her," he said abruptly. "I wanted to help her before that crazy life destroyed her. Such a fragile, delicate child— My God, she reminded me of my own dear mother at that age. I took her to my apartment just to get her off the street. She was the daughter I never had."

I didn't understand if it was his dear old mother or the daughter he never had who he wanted to tie him to the bedpost, but that wasn't my problem.

"Where is she, Giles?"

"I don't know. But I can help you. I've got a reporter I'll loan you. Brilliant guy; he'll find her."

I shook my head. A reporter digging into Bonnie's life was the last thing I wanted. Giles nodded craftily; he understood. "Don't worry. He'll be like a private detective assigned to help you. Grady, I care about this girl."

Before I could stop him, he was on the phone, and seconds later a tough-looking, square-jawed man with a broken nose and a wing of dark hair flopping in his eyes strode into the office. He glared at Giles, then at me, clearly not happy with our company. He had a crazed look in his eye, too. Was everybody at this great journal insane?

"Grady Malloy, Sid Banks. You must know Sid's byline, the prizes he's won. Unfortunately he's got a legal problem right now, and time on his hands. Sid, Grady is a dear friend of mine who needs our help. He'll explain."

The reporter glared at his editor, then at me, with

100

undisguised loathing; if looks could kill, it would have been a double murder. I'd never seen two people I more wanted to escape. It was like stumbling into a Pinter play and finding yourself trapped by unattractive people who hate you for unexplained reasons. I said I'd call the reporter and fled to the relative safety of midtown Manhattan.

11

I returned to the Waldorf and gave my driver the night off. Up in my borrowed luxury suite I ate a sandwich and called home. Linda had talked to Penny, but no one had heard from Bonnie.

God knows I didn't want to go out again, but I couldn't waste the evening. There was a movie director listed in Bonnie's notebook, a man whose work I'd admired for years. Her notes said, "He just wants three or four girls—the younger the better—to come and put on kimonos and dance for him. Then he'll pose us, like he's making a movie, and when he's tired of that he talks about how Hollywood used to be. He's really sweet and he's got this great apartment— two Oscars on the mantel—but it's sad, too. He's got granddaughters my age, but he never sees them, and he says he's too old for sex. He's sweet but so lonely and sad."

Might Bonnie have sought refuge with him?

Maybe, but I wasn't up to confronting a lonely old man that evening.

Instead, I caught a cab to Ruth Orlando's brownstone.

She met me at the door, an enchantress with soft hands and dancing eyes. But all I could see was Monica, greeting me two weeks earlier. Monica had been lovely, too, and someone had blown her brains out.

Ruth guided me inside. "I'm so glad you came," she murmured. I wondered what she took me for. Some horny fool who couldn't get laid?

Monica's apartment had been huge and dramatic; Ruth's was small and intimate. Two connected drawing rooms with fireplaces, sconces and candles, leather chairs, soft music—Sarah Vaughan's "Stella by Starlight"—as I entered. A bartender passing around drinks and hot hors d'oeuvres. And perhaps fourteen or fifteen people scattered about, young women and middle-aged men, the candlelight creating an illusion of privacy.

We settled on an ornate antique sofa, and the bartender brought champagne. Ruth brushed back her ash-blonde hair. The candlelight was cosmetic; it softened her profile, touched her with magic. "Are you comfortable?" she asked.

"More than you know."

"I'm glad. People deserve moments of pure pleasure."

"And you provide them?"

"I provide a setting. Ultimately pleasure comes from within."

"It's like a drug," I said. "I feel high."

I was flattering her, but it was true, too. After that scene with Giles Kessler, this was heaven.

"Love is the ultimate drug," Ruth said.

"Love or sex?"

"I like to think the two are closely related. Don't you?"

I shrugged. "In the long haul, the challenge is to live happily with one person."

I have a perverse habit of sticking up for monogamy. Once, while a guest at the Playboy mansion, I tried to persuade Hugh Hefner that marriage is a higher state of existence than bedding an endless succession of twenty-year-old girls. Hef, bless him, just chuckled and said, "You don't understand. I tried marriage, and it didn't work."

"Granted," Ruth said with a serpentine smile. "I deal in illusions. But sex with someone you may never see again can be a moment of beauty, of perfection, a memory that never dies. I like making that happen. I think of myself as being in the pleasure business."

I smiled, for I liked the phrase, and it occurred to me that I'm in the pleasure business, too, although a different branch of it. Alas, the world was a lot more interested in her product than mine.

She took my hand and seemed quite content to

sit there listening to Chris Connor sing "Spring Is Here." I hated to break the spell.

"May I ask you an unpleasant question?"

"You hardly look capable of it, Grady."

"I knew Monica Wilcox. You know what happened to her. Doesn't it frighten you?"

For an instant her face grew cold; then she smiled wanly. "Planes crash, but we keep on flying, don't we?"

I thought that an idiotic analogy—we were talking about cold-blooded murder, not plane crashes—but before I could frame a reply, the bartender came and whispered to Ruth. She turned to me. "Excuse me," she said. "It's someone I must greet. Make yourself absolutely at home. Meet some of the girls—if you don't mind making me jealous."

She moved away, and I stayed on the sofa, happy to be in the shadows, silent and watching. The women were all beautiful, and there was one Eurasian girl who was not to be believed. The men were prosperous-looking fellows in their forties and early fifties. An ugly little red-haired lawyer was bragging to a girl about a libel judgment he'd won, and a tall, patrician man was talking about a skyscraper he was designing. The women listened well and smiled exquisitely; was this what we men wanted, even more than sex—simply the illusion of being adored by gorgeous young women?

Two couples were dancing in the back room. The song was "For All We Know," and it reminded me of a girl in Tennessee long ago. When the young woman came out of the shadows and settled beside me, I didn't recognize her at first. She had traded her "So Many Men" T-shirt for something dark and shimmering.

"I'm Annette," she said.

"Yes."

I didn't know what to say after that. I was still remembering the time I danced with the girl to "For All We Know" in the shadows of a spooky Victorian mansion before a boy who loved her killed himself and she went to Paris to forget the unpleasantry. Lost between past and present, I looked at this very different girl and said, "Dance?"

She led me to the shadowy back room. Annette was a big, strong girl with broad shoulders, yet wonderfully light in my arms. To hold her like that was to imagine doing many things with her, but asking her questions was not among them.

"I've seen you somewhere," she said.

"At Monica's. I was Bonnie . . . Blair's friend."

I felt her body stiffen, but I had to keep on. "I'm trying to find her. Can you help me?"

"No." The song was over. We stood facing each other.

"Where would she hide?"

"I don't know. I don't want to know."

"She was your friend. Don't you care what happens to her? What are you afraid of?"

"Get me a drink," she said. "Bourbon."

I got her the drink, and we returned to the sofa. She began to talk, and I leaned close to listen.

"I hate it because I got her into this. The money looks so good at first. You don't know, you can't imagine, all the crap that goes with it. Even Monica didn't know. It's like a bottomless pit. Down, down, down."

She lowered her head. I took one of her hands. I didn't want her to cry; I was desperate to keep her talking. "Where were you from, Annette? Before New York?"

She laughed bitterly. "Me? Oh, I'm an American classic. A preacher's daughter from Nebraska who wound up on her back. I came here to be an actress. Most of the girls did. Auditions, lessons, waitressing, waiting, hoping, dreaming, starving. Then somebody offers you easy money. You know why I'm a whore? Because I'm too damn honest. I owed so many people money, and the only way I could pay them back was by working for Monica. So I started having dates, and I paid my debts, except pretty soon I had bigger debts because I got hung up on cocaine. I couldn't stand prosperity."

"Annette, who killed Monica?"

I'd hoped to jolt the truth out of her, but she was past my jolting.

"I don't know. I just want to survive. Too many people are asking questions. I'm leaving town. There's a lawyer in there; he just won a big case, and he's going to give me money, and I'm going somewhere and wait for him."

"That night at Monica's, when the Arabs were there, did they say anything about . . . about Israeli security or why Khalid Yassin was coming or about a cassette?"

"I never listened to them. It was boring, all oil and politics."

She twisted nervously. I was losing her. "Annette, who would she turn to? Where would she hide?"

"Her boyfriend? Maybe she . . ." Then she gasped, eyes wide, and I followed her gaze and saw the big ape I'd seen outside Monica's apartment. Nicky Allegro, Bonnie had called him. He was at the bar, his back to me, but you couldn't mistake those shoulders, that bulk, the sinister sheen of his beard. He radiated power and menace; I saw the careful way the bartender regarded him and how the others in the room had subtly shifted, first looking at him and then turning away. Annette pressed close to me, trembling, trying to hide behind me.

"Who is he?"

"Don't ask. Really."

"Bonnie knew him. He might know where she is."

"Pray to God that he doesn't." She hurried to the

lawyer in the front room, a short, ugly cherub with red hair and fuzzy sideburns. She whispered to him, and he left the Eurasian girl and followed her into the hallway.

My every instinct was to confront Nick Allegro —could that be his real name?—to demand that he tell me where Bonnie was, to try to bluff him, frighten him. And yet I held back. Would my Washington connections impress him? Would anything impress him except a shotgun to his gut? Would my fear render me speechless? I was sitting in the shadows; I could see him without being seen. I heard him bantering with the bartender about the next Giants game; the bartender crooned, "Yeah, right, Mr. Allegro."

The drug dealer nodded absently and dipped one hamlike hand into the peanut bowl. He was wearing a gorgeous camel's hair overcoat that fit like a glove; there was a stunning contrast between his elegant clothing and the brutal, primordial set of his features. His coal-black beard was perfectly trimmed, Mephistophelian.

Again, I wanted to confront him but hesitated. If I had any advantage, it was that he didn't know me.

Allegro crossed the room to the Eurasian girl. The man with her backed away. She held her smile.

I saw Annette and the red-haired lawyer hurry out the front door. After a moment I went to a window and saw them standing beside a taxi. She kissed him and slipped into the cab. The lawyer stood there a long time, the back of his hand to his mouth, watching the cab disappear, as the November wind whipped leaves down the street. I wondered if he wanted to leave his wife for her and how much it would cost him and what would happen to the preacher's daughter turned would-be actress turned coked-up whore.

Such speculations were my true concern—the fragments of life that are the stuff of fiction—not this insane wild-goose chase I had embarked on. What I had learned that long day was that I was far over my head. Let the police and Harry Prescott worry about Bonnie and Monica and the Arabs, the whole damn mess. It wasn't my business. At best I was wasting my time, and at worst I was risking my life.

As I watched from the window, Nick Allegro suddenly charged out the door to the street. The lawyer who'd bidden good-bye to Annette was about to enter a cab. Allegro seized him by the collar, lifted him off the ground, poured abuse on him, then tossed him aside like a rag doll. The lawyer lay twitching in the gutter as the drug dealer climbed into the cab.

I started for the door to help the lawyer, but I was stopped by a gentle hand on my arm.

"Let it be," Ruth Orlando said. We watched as the lawyer picked himself up and hobbled down the street, with leaves dancing at his heels.

"He'll be all right," Ruth said. "It's been a long, difficult day. I'm just glad Nicky exploded out there instead of in here. The man is a walking time bomb."

"Why do you let him in?"

Her wide mouth twisted into a bitter smile. "Because I can't keep him out. My God, I need a drink. Or something. Would you come upstairs with me? The world is so much nicer there."

I didn't doubt there were rare joys to be found upstairs. I was drawn by Ruth's beauty and her cynicism and her mystery. But I couldn't climb those stairs. When I was younger, I believed you could do anything, have it all, but I've seen too many disasters, too much heartbreak. Two-thirds of the men I grew up with are on their second or third marriage and have kids who won't speak to them, and a lot of them are dead or in jail or in mental institutions or battling addictions of one sort or another. I think there's a rough justice in the world and if you break the rules long enough, the rules will break you. So I fled Ruth's pleasure dome, not because I was high-minded; only because I was scared, only because I want to hold on to what I've got.

I caught a cab back to the Waldorf. All I wanted was ten hours' sleep and a seat on the shuttle back to home, back to sanity.

I unlocked the door to Orth Butler's sanctuary, thinking how big and empty the bed would be, and as I fumbled for the light, a voice floated out of the darkness.

"Good evening, Mr. Malloy."

12

The light came on, and I saw a silver-haired man on the sofa and a younger man standing behind him. They were wearing tuxedos—the older man had his jacket on, and the younger man's was off—and for an instant I thought they might be friends of Orth Butler, dropped by for a drink. Then I realized that friends wouldn't have waited in the dark.

I turned and found another one, tall and tough and unsmiling, behind me, foiling my escape plan, so I asked the silver-haired one, "Who are you?"

He stood up. He was wiry and tanned, with a weathered face, thick dark eyebrows, and his wavy hair trimmed short. I thought he'd have been more comfortable in khaki.

"Consider us your friends," the man said. I saw the younger men's jackets hanging over two dining-room chairs. Perhaps the tuxedos had helped them slip past the supposedly impregnable security of the Waldorf Towers.

"What do you want?"

"To speak with you," the man said. "And to obtain the missing cassette."

At least there was no bullshit about him. "I don't have it," I said.

"Still we must search."

"Be my guest."

"Thank you. Perhaps you and I could have a drink while we talk."

That was civilized enough. I poured brandy for us both. We settled on facing leather sofas while the younger men pursued their search, using long needles to probe cushions and mattresses, and small metal detectors. I saw a certain humor in this meticulous search for something I knew wasn't there. "Do you really think you could find a cassette in this huge apartment?"

The man chuckled. "Mr. Malloy, you could conceal a dime in Grand Central Station and those young men would find it in ten minutes."

I thought about that, then said, "Are you Palmach?"

He shrugged. "Names change. We are devoted to the cause of Israel."

"And what is the cause of Israel?"

"To survive."

I thought of Annette, just an hour earlier, saying that all she wanted was to survive. It was a universal fantasy. I thought of a poem about a graveyard: "Then depart, but see ye tread, / Lightly, lightly, o'er the dead."

"From all I hear, Israel is doing well these days."

The man's weathered face suggested both vitality and weariness. "Mr. Malloy, how much do you know about the Middle Eastern situation?"

I shrugged. "Not much."

"Are you indifferent to it?"

He was a serious man, and my instinct was to give serious answers. "No, not indifferent. But I avoid the issue. It all seems so damn hopeless. It's like people made mistakes fifty or a hundred years ago and now there's no answer, no alternative, to endless bloodshed."

He tasted his brandy for the first time.

"No offense intended," I added.

"None taken. There is truth in what you say. Are you familiar with Theodor Herzl?"

"No."

"He was a Viennese journalist, the father of Zionism. He had observed the Dreyfus affair and concluded that Jews could never live unmolested in Europe and must therefore create a nation of their own. Herzl's vision was thus both nationalistic and revolutionary, with few precedents in human history. Zionists were required to leave behind their homes, their languages, their cultures, and begin new lives in a distant, hostile land. One must seek comparisons with the Crusades, or perhaps your Pilgrims."

He ventured another sip of brandy. I heard the two young men whispering in one of the bedrooms.

"Herzl's little book, *Der Judenstaat*, 'The Jewish State,' was published in 1896. At that point he had no specific location in mind. The new state might have been in Canada or Argentina or Africa. Only gradually did the idea of Palestine take hold, but it held great emotional appeal. For Jews to return to their Biblical homeland was such a beautiful dream that hardly anyone stopped to think that there were already people living in Palestine."

"Are you saying Canada would have been a better decision?"

"Without question. But the point is moot. Palestine was chosen, so we face the present reality of three million Israelis surrounded by one hundred and fifty million Arabs whose stated goal is their military destruction."

"Isn't there a good deal of rhetorical overkill in that?"

"Is there? Forgive a personal note, Mr. Malloy. I was born in Germany. My father was a banker. When Hitler came to power, my father understood him. His friends laughed. They said Hitler was only another blustering politician. But my father took the Brownshirts seriously. He sold everything, and we sailed to Palestine. Life was not easy there. But in five years we were alive and our friends in Germany were dead. I am not an optimist about human nature, Mr. Malloy. I take the Arabs at their word."

"Tell me your name."

"You may call me Uri."

"Why are you telling me all this?"

"For two reasons. First, you write for Senator Prescott, who could be president. We would be grateful if you focused more closely on our situation."

"As you probably know, the senator has several people who do little except focus on your situation. What's the second reason?"

"You have become involved, apparently by accident, in the matter of the cassette."

"Entirely by accident. I wish I'd never heard of the damn thing. But now that you mention it, what's on it?"

He took a third sip. My glass was empty. "More?"

"No thank you."

I filled my glass and sat down again. "The cassette—what's on it?"

Uri gazed down his long nose at me. "I have no idea. Only fears and suspicions."

"Which are?"

"Mr. Malloy . . ."

"Grady, please."

"Grady, we are not surrounded by a monolithic 'Arab world' but by dozens of nations and factions. Some are relatively sane, and some are utterly irrational, people who have sworn to drive us into the sea and are willing to die in that cause. We are well armed and better soldiers than our enemies, but in a nuclear age we can take nothing for granted."

I was impressed by Uri and yet skeptical of what he was saying. I once worked on a speech that a presidential candidate delivered to a gathering of rich New York Jews, and it was one of the worst experiences of my life. Those people have a party line, and if you don't toe it, they'll chop you to pieces. They're fierce people, and give-and-take isn't part of their political philosophy.

"You're the ones with the bomb, aren't you?"

He didn't bother with the fiction that Israel lacks a nuclear capacity. "Yes, but we can never rule out the possibility that some Arab nation or faction will obtain a nuclear device. Suppose Qaddafi buys one? Or the PLO steals one? What then? You're the novelist; you write the scenario. Suppose an unmarked plane drops a nuclear weapon on Tel Aviv. Do we retaliate with nuclear weapons? Against whom? Would our retaliation only play into the hands of our rejectionist enemies, giving them an excuse for a massive invasion? Or is the invasion coming no matter what we do? Could that one stolen weapon, dropped from an unmarked plane, lead to the second Holocaust? Fiction to you, perhaps, but questions we must address with the utmost seriousness."

"So what about the cassette?" I pressed.

Uri shook his head wearily. "We hear many rumors, most of them false. A current one, which has elements of probability, concerns a plan for the use of a nuclear device to trigger a massive invasion by certain radical factions. I assume Khalid Yassin heard the same reports. When he made an unscheduled trip to your country, we were most curious. What is on the cassette? It would be unusual for anything so sensitive to be put on tape or on paper. But perhaps it is highly technical material. Perhaps it is an intercepted message that proves the intent of the conspirators. Who knows? I had hoped to find out from Yassin one way or another, but I moved too slowly."

The young men came and stood beside Uri's chair. One of them spoke to him in a language I didn't understand. The other one produced my revolver—he made some sort of joke about it—and put it on the table. He had Bonnie's two notebooks, too; I'd "hidden" them under my socks. They went and started searching the kitchen.

"You're saying you didn't kill the Arabs and the women," I persisted.

"Whoever did that was twice a fool, for the senseless slaughter and for letting the girl escape with the cassette."

"Who was it?" I asked. "Who killed them?"

"It was a crude, ugly piece of work. The PLO is capable of that, and various Islamic splinter groups, as well as your domestic criminal elements."

I was starting to have questions. Uri was a charming fellow, but how much did he know? Where was he getting his information? From the police? Or somewhere else?

As if reading my thoughts, he said, "We seek the girl who escaped, or rather the cassette we believe she took with her. You seem to have knowledge of her."

"I happened to meet her a few weeks ago. She was a young call girl. Blair, she called herself; I never knew her last name. I was interested in her story, as a writer. She took me to Monica's apartment one evening, and when I read about the murders, I was afraid she'd been killed. So I came up to see if I could help the police."

By now I felt like a fool whenever I told my story, but I was stuck with it.

"And how did you know about the cassette?" Uri asked.

I groped for an answer, for there was no way in hell I was going to volunteer information about my daughter's friendship with Bonnie. I saw now that two forces, at least two, were searching for the cassette, and the other one had pursued Bonnie to Charlottesville, but Uri apparently didn't know about that.

"The police," I said. "They asked me about the cassette."

He cocked an eyebrow, then picked up Bonnie's date book and began to study it. "She gave that to me," I said. "To give me some specifics if I wanted to write about her. Make a copy of it, if you think it'll help you."

He continued to study the book. Finally, he said, "You visited one of these men today."

I didn't bother to ask how he knew. "The editor, yes. He says he has no idea where she is."

Uri called one of the others. The young man sat down nearby and began copying from the two notebooks.

"I'll make you a deal," I told Uri. "If you find the girl, bring her to me. If I find the cassette, I'll give it to you. Okay?"

"Of course." He gingerly examined my cheap little revolver as he might a dead mouse. "A word of advice. If you wish to go armed, go armed. A weapon is of little use hidden beneath your socks."

"I'll remember that."

The other young man came out of the kitchen empty-handed. It was my turn to laugh. "If I had the cassette, would I bring it here? Wouldn't I hide it at home?"

"Your home was searched this afternoon."

"You sons of bitches."

"Your wife was away. She is at present one of the safest women in America."

"You mean you're watching my house?"

He ignored the question, having already answered it. "If you would be so good as to stand and remove your coat."

I was more amused than angry. It reminded me of the scene in *The Maltese Falcon* when Bogart gives Peter Lorre his gun back, then Lorre insists on searching him, anyway. Not that Uri was anything like Peter Lorre or I much of a Bogart. One of the young men patted me down, quickly and expertly, then stepped back.

"How do I get in touch with you?" I asked.

He gave me a slip of paper. "Call this number and give your name and location. We are finished now. Thank you for your cooperation."

We shook hands and they were gone. I could have picked up the phone and had them arrested in the lobby—or would they have easily dispatched the Waldorf's security guards?—but there was no point in it. Uri looked like a good friend to have. My own position seemed increasingly hopeless. If I told all I knew, it could shatter Bonnie's life, not to mention Harry's campaign. But as long as I held back the truth, I might have God knows what sinister forces pursuing me.

My plans remained unchanged despite Uri's visit: a good night's sleep and an early flight home. A strategic retreat, you could call it, or a coward's way out. Call it what you like, I'd had enough.

13

For breakfast I ordered fresh orange juice, strawberries, a small fillet, poached eggs, hash browns, buttered toast, coffee, and—the crowning touch—a split of Dom Perignon. Orth Butler could afford it.

Thus refreshed, I left the hotel in midmorning and emerged into a cold, nasty rain. I dodged a couple of umbrellas, wielded by women whose clear goal was to blind me, and scanned Park Avenue for a cab.

To my delight, one eased around the corner. I waved both arms, and it whizzed past an elderly gentleman and stopped for yours truly. My lucky day, I decided, and climbed into the backseat.

"La Guardia," I said, and unfolded my *Times*. I used to second-guess New York cabbies, afraid they were cheating me, demanding that they take this bridge or that tunnel, but I no longer wanted to fight that hard for four or five dollars. Soon I was thinking about what Uri had said. Could there be an Arab plot to destroy Israel? Was that what was on that damned cassette?

Hell no, I told myself. Probably the cassette, if it was ever found, would contain an old Benny Goodman concert—weren't all Arab princes crazy for Benny Goodman? I wasn't worrying about it anymore. NMP, not my problem.

We were moving uptown, playing stop-and-go amid sheets of rain. I half noticed as we made a couple of quick turns, then looked up as we stopped under an overpass. It was dark there, and I wondered if we were lost. I looked up and saw the driver's shadowy eyes in the mirror. I was framing a question when both rear doors flew open and two men leaped in.

Things happened very fast after that. I raised my arms. Both invaders pounded my gut. I doubled up; then one of them pinned my arms while the other one played a solo number on my rib cage. I was grunting and squirming, and all I saw was that they were dark-skinned and one was older than the other—thirty and twenty, maybe. I was nauseous, close to passing out, when they tossed me onto the street and one began kicking me while the other rummaged through my bag.

My guts were exploding, and they'd done a job on my kidneys, too. All I could do was curl into a ball and cover my head and groan. The older one spoke to the one who was kicking me, then knelt beside me, checked my pockets with nimble fingers, and hissed, "Go home, asshole!"

He found my revolver, laughed, and tossed it into some weeds, then jumped into the cab. I wondered if they were going to run over me. Instead, they roared away, leaving me half-dead in the gutter.

I mumbled and moaned for a while, but the world took no notice of my plight. While struggling to my knees, I unburdened myself of my hundred-dollar breakfast. A couple of urchins eyed me from across the street. I cried for help, but their mother called them away. Slowly I stood up, my poor insides howling, and gathered my clothes from the street. The pouring rain only added to my misery. I retrieved my gun, too. I hadn't had much luck with it, but I was sustained by a fantasy in which I blew those two bastards to hell.

I spit blood and realized my cut lip was from my fall; they hadn't hit my face, only my body.

I leaned against a pole and looked for help. I didn't even know where I was; in a downpour somewhere near the East River. A cab came along, and the driver took one look at me and ran the stop sign. I wasn't a pretty sight, plus my arms and legs weren't working right. Another cab came by, and I stepped in front of it. The driver reluctantly chose to stop rather than run me down, and I jerked open the door and muttered, "Take me to the Waldorf. I've been mugged!"

Yes, even in my distress I recognized a good line when I spoke it.

I caused something of a stir when I staggered wet, bloody, and filthy through Peacock Alley, but I persuaded an assistant manager to call a doctor and readmit me to Orth's apartment. The doctor, a young fellow with a bushy beard, poked me over and said, "This was no mugging."

He was right, of course. Somebody had told those thugs, "Give him a five"—a five, on their ten scale, being a working over that spares the face, inflicts no permanent damage, yet causes enough pain to encourage serious consideration of the message being sent.

In this case: "Go home, asshole!"

You bastards, I was trying to go home!

The doctor gave me some Percodan, urged me to stay in bed a couple of days, and said to call him if I pissed blood for more than twenty-four hours. When he left, I took a double dose of Percodan, washed it down with beer, and began to rethink my day.

I wanted more than ever to go home but wasn't sure I could manage the flight. The shuttle was no place to stagger, drool, and piss blood. I was thinking I might ask Linda to fly up when the phone rang. It was agony to hear it, to lift the receiver, to croak a hello. The man at the desk whispered that a Mr. Sidney Banks wished to see me.

I said I didn't know any Sidney Banks.

"He says he's a reporter," the desk clerk added.

Then I remembered. Sid Banks, the investigative reporter whom Giles Kessler had graciously assigned to me.

I groaned yet again. I didn't trust Giles, and I didn't trust Sid Banks, either. Nor did I want anyone to see me in this shape.

And yet there was something else. I was in more mental and physical pain than I'd ever known before. I was lonely and scared, and, yes, misery does love company, even the company of a wild-eyed investigative reporter.

"Send the gentleman up," I said.

14

There exists in political lore a cherished form of attire known as the Full Cleveland: white leisure suit, white belt, white socks and shoes, white tie, plus an optional electric blue, chocolate, or flamingo-pink shirt. Sid Banks arrived wearing what I can only call a Full Newsroom: shapeless dark suit, pale blue wash-and-wear shirt with its collar unbuttoned, a narrow, obscenely stained striped tie out of the fifties, sagging white socks, and what must have been his old army shoes. There's a new breed of reporters today who dress like stockbrokers, but Sid was vintage Front Page, a blast from the past.

He greeted me with a scowl, then brightened when he saw the bar. When he had a full glass in hand, he took a chair opposite mine and barked, "What happened to you?"

"A couple of thugs beat me up."

"I know some thugs. Describe them."

I could have been describing a million guys. Sid

shook his head. "You'd have to give me more to go on."

My insides hurt too much for tact. "I'm not sure I want to give you anything. I don't trust Giles, and I don't know why I should trust you."

"Suit yourself." He downed half his drink. "Giles said to help you if you wanted help."

"What else did he tell you?"

"That you were looking for some whore. That you were old buddies and he wanted to do you a favor."

"Do you believe that?"

Sid killed his drink in one graceful motion, tipping the glass straight up lest a single drop escape him. The only other man I ever saw tilt a glass quite so boldly was Stephen Spender, with whom Sid otherwise had little in common.

The reporter shrugged. "I know you're not old buddies. But it doesn't matter. I expect Giles to lie."

"What is it with you two?" I remembered reading a news story about Sid Banks a year or so before.

"It's simple. He hates my guts, and I hate his. But we're stuck with each other because some scumbag governor sued us for libel. So he took me off reporting. I spend my time giving depositions. Holding the hands of idiot lawyers. If Giles says to help you, it's a way to get out of the office."

He helped himself to more scotch and ice.

"But you'll report back to him?"

Sid looked annoyed. "Look, I told you, I hate his guts, but I've got nothing against you."

As I hobbled over to pour myself a stiff drink, he added, "For what it's worth, I know your stuff; some of it's not bad. I remember when you used to write for magazines. I never figured why you switched to books."

"Economics. You can starve writing for magazines. Plus the editors are all idiots."

"And book editors aren't?"

"You deal with fewer of them."

He shrugged, unpersuaded. "You write magazine articles, you screw other people; you write books, other people screw you."

The man was not without certain insights. I'd known other reporters like Sid. Stubborn, surly, sloppy sons of bitches who make lousy husbands and erratic employees but who have a dedication to truth, as they define it, not unlike that of crusaders to the Holy Grail. My instinct was to trust him, up to a point.

I told him most of the story, but omitting what Uri had said might be on the cassette and that the missing girl was Harry Prescott's daughter.

When I finished, Sid was stretched out on the floor with his shoes off, tugging at his grimy socks. "Pal, you're in big trouble," he announced.

"Tell me something I don't know."

Sid dialed a soap opera on the TV, full volume, and pulled his chair close to mine.

"Let's talk about whores," he said. "Monica, Ruth, all the rest of them."

"Blair called them madams. She said she knew six or eight like that."

"There's hundreds. It's the East Side's leading cottage industry. A girl like Monica, she starts off peddling her ass. She can average three hundred a pop. Maybe only two from her regulars, but four or five from the weirdos. How many pops a week? She could manage twenty if she wanted to, but let's be conservative. Let's say ten a week. That's three thousand bucks a week, a hundred and fifty thousand a year, cash, tax-free, for screwing less than your average newlywed. Sweet, huh?"

"Sure. A million laughs."

"Pretty soon she's got more guys lined up outside her door than she can handle. So she calls in a friend to help. Then two or three friends. Say there's four of them fucking ten times a week at three hundred per; that's six hundred thousand bucks a year. Sounds too good to be true, doesn't it?"

I nodded my agreement. My ribs were throbbing. The doctor said they weren't broken, but he might have lied.

"Well, it is too good to be true. Wake up, Malloy. This is the Big Apple. We don't let Monica clear a half mil a year because she's a nice kid with a sweet ass. That's not how things work. Somebody moves in."

"The mob." I wondered why I hadn't thought of it before. I'd been living out in the country too long, out where a stolen bicycle is a crime wave.

"Right. One day a wise guy in pinstripes knocks on the door and says, 'Honey, I'm your new partner. I give you protection, sell you drugs wholesale, and take half your profits. If you don't like my offer, I break your jaw.' He breaks a few jaws, and word gets around that this is a serious businessman. So Monica pays up and keeps her profile intact."

"It stinks," I said.

" 'Twas ever thus. The thing is, it's not the mob that interests me here. What gets me about Monica's setup, was all the foreigners—Arabs, Israelis, Japs. It's like she was trying to bang the whole damn UN."

As Sid spoke, he was trimming his toenails with a hunting knife he'd pulled from his pocket.

"A lot of foreign businessmen come to New York."

"A lot of foreign politicians, too, and they all want to dip their peckers in the local honey pot. The mob doesn't care about foreigners, just cash flow, but there's folks out there who do care about foreigners."

"The CIA."

"You got it. They want to keep tabs on the Arabs, the Jews, everybody, and what better time than when

131

they've got their pants down? You said the girl hid in a room where Monica meant to put a camera but never did. Who says she never did?"

"Are you saying the CIA would know who killed those people?"

Sid picked thoughtfully at his big toe. "Who the hell knows? The CIA's got more factions than the PLO. Some pro-Israel, some pro-Arab. Any food in this dump?"

I waved him into the kitchen. He returned in a minute with a sandwich; I hoped he'd washed his hands. "I didn't mention it, but the night I left Monica's, we saw this big ox with a black beard, Nick Allegro; Blair said he was a dealer. Then, at Ruth Orlando's, I saw him again. Annette was scared to death of him."

Sid chewed his sandwich. "She ought to be. Nicky is an evil son of a bitch. He's Mr. Cocaine, until somebody kills him. A couple of years ago, the mob cut a deal with all the crazy free-lance Colombians who'd been bringing coke in. It was Nicky who made the deal—killed four or five of the Colombians and reasoned with the survivors."

"Blair said she'd been to his apartment. She said there were Colombians there with suitcases full of cocaine."

"Sure. The call-girl racket and the cocaine business fit together like ham and eggs. The girls get hooked, the johns like a little toot, and it's a sweet way to retail the stuff with no risks. Nicky can make deliveries and be a big man with the chippies, too. There's some real ugly stories about him and girls."

Things were getting too complicated. All I wanted was Bonnie, not an international drug conspiracy. But I remembered that Penny said the guys who broke into her dorm spoke Spanish, and the guys who beat me up spoke it, too. "Does Allegro have Colombians working for him?"

"Sure. He's an equal-opportunity employer."

"Then he's the key to the whole damn thing," I said.

The phone interrupted me. I turned down the TV and answered. "I heard you had an accident," Lee Draper said.

"Bad news travels fast."

"The hotel called because you're in Orth's suite. Look, the senator wants you to join him for dinner tonight."

"I don't think I can travel," I told him.

"We can make it easy. A limo picks you up there and takes you to Orth's plane at the Marine Air Terminal. You want a doctor aboard to hold your hand? You fly to National; then another limo takes you to the senator's office. How about it?"

"Have cold beer and Percodan on the plane. No doctor."

"Done."

"When can the limo be ready?"

"When can you be ready? It's downstairs."

I didn't give a damn about dinner with Harry Prescott, but it was a smooth voyage home. "I'm leaving," I told Sid Banks. "Somebody just made me an offer I couldn't refuse."

"Who?" he asked suspiciously.

"Do you know a man named Lee Draper?"

Sid snickered nastily but didn't reply. I didn't press him; I wasn't planning ever to see Lee Draper again.

"What are you going to do?" Sid asked.

"I don't know. Either I'll go home and forget all about this mess, or I'll get madder and madder and come back up here and blow Allegro's ugly head off."

"Don't try it. He's a tough boy, and he's got other tough boys backing him up. Do you want me to do some digging?"

"Sure," I said. "But don't worry about drugs or the CIA or that crap. Just find the girl. No offense, but if you found her, I think her family would be very generous."

"Money never offends me," he said. "Only the bastards that have it."

He left, and I hobbled into the bathroom, peed a glorious shade of pink, and went to pack my things.

15

The moment I entered Harry's office, Amanda pounced on me like a tiger.

"You sleazy yellow-dog son of a bitch," she began. "You despicable turd. You . . ."

She went on like that, and she wasn't bad for a Sweetbriar girl. Fortunately I was too full of booze and Percodan to take it personally. I leaned against Harry's desk, grinning inanely at this charming creature whom I might help elevate to first lady of the land.

At forty, Amanda was petite and ripe, with reddish hair, flashing eyes, and a delicate China-doll complexion. She was dressed to the nines, in vivid tangerine silk, with a dramatic black-and-white Hermes scarf and a not-quite-vulgar display of diamonds.

As she eloquently denounced my mother, my manhood, and my mental state, I recalled an evening years before. Someone on our block was having a

TGIF party, the big, noisy kind where people drank too much jug wine and made out with each other's spouses. It was that final Watergate summer, and everyone in Washington was a little crazed.

I happened to have a couple of joints, the gift of some kids I'd met in an antiwar march. Harry and Linda didn't approve of the stuff, but around midnight Amanda whispered, "Let's get high," and lured me out to her car. We smoked the joints, and then we sat there listening to "Abbey Road" float across the lawn and feeling one with the universe.

After a while, Amanda whispered, "Kiss me." She sounded almost humble, a way she'd never sounded before, and it seemed a reasonable request, a spark of human warmth in a vast and uncaring solar system, so I kissed her and marveled at how soft her mouth was, that in some mysterious way her mouth and the universe were truly one. Clearly, mine were cosmic thoughts, but Amanda's mind was more precisely focused. She surprised me by reaching for my fly, and she kept on surprising me until I chanced to open my eyes and see Harry marching toward us.

"Oh, boy," I sighed, but Amanda was as cool as the proverbial cucumber. In one graceful motion she righted herself, deftly arranged her clothing, and sweetly informed Harry that she and I were having a serious talk about my problems with Linda. He apologized for the intrusion and hurriedly withdrew.

Amanda never sought to rekindle our brief moment of togetherness, but I was tempted to remind her of it now, as she continued to inform me, via various metaphorical flights, that I was lower than snake shit. No doubt she would have claimed I drugged her and tried to rape her.

She had completed her preamble and was getting down to specifics: "You meet secretly with my daughter in New York, you *know* she's fallen into bad company, but do you tell her mother? No, you rat fucker, you leave the poor child alone and helpless to become involved in a murder—a *murder*, for Christ's sake—and then . . ."

When she came up for air, I said, "Where's Harry?"

"Don't get smart with me, Grady Malloy. I know you. You never did have any morals!"

I grew impatient. Despite the various drugs, the pain in my guts was growing worse.

"Dammit, Amanda, Harry asked me to dinner. Where the hell is he?"

"Don't curse at me!"

"Look, I just got back from New York. I was looking for Bonnie. Two guys beat me up."

"I wish they'd killed you."

The door flew open, and her husband and my wife burst in. "Surprise!" Harry cried.

Linda hugged me; that was the drug I needed. Then Amanda hugged Linda, saying, "My darling, wherever have you been?"

Harry didn't hug me, but he was all smiles. He'd blasted the CIA in a hearing that afternoon, and his remarks had made the network news. "Let's celebrate!" he declared. "A long-awaited reunion." He produced a bottle of champagne. Soon toasts to the good old days filled the air.

With the arrival of the others, Amanda had become all sweetness and light; the Wicked Witch was miraculously Snow White again. Poor preoccupied Harry didn't know the difference. When we finished the champagne, Harry asked if he should have dinner brought to the office. I said I'd rather go out—I wanted people around in case Amanda grew violent—so we walked over to the Monocle.

The restaurant was crowded with congressmen and lobbyists and other low types, but we were quickly ushered to a secluded table. The only problem with our little party was that the shadow of their missing daughter hung over it. I'd learned nothing in New York, nothing I could repeat, and when we got around to that topic, it might be a grim reunion.

But Amanda was way ahead of me. We'd no sooner sat down than she announced, "Oh, by the way, darling, I have the most wonderful news. Bonnie called. She has a job with an advertising agency, and she'll be home for Thanksgiving and start back to college in January."

Harry was stunned. "You didn't tell me."

"Darling, you're never home to tell."

For a moment I believed her, because I wanted to believe her; then I realized she'd made it all up rather than admit she hadn't any idea where her daughter was. The boldness of her lie was breathtaking. And later she'd invent another lie to explain away the first one.

But at least her lie made our dinner less tense than it might have been. With Bonnie accounted for, we relaxed and told tales of the old days in Cleveland Park, and Harry loosened up and was the funny, charming man he can be when he's not saving the world.

It was impressive to watch him, because I knew what it meant to run for president. I knew what a vast and maddening equation he carried in his mind of people, money, issues, image, organization, timing, tactics, and yet he was able to put it aside and laugh about parties and picnics and softball games fifteen years before. For an instant I liked him again; politics hadn't yet turned him into a machine. Harry had us all helpless with laughter as he recalled a long-ago game of charades when, because of my nasty mind, he'd had to act out "If you can't get a woman get a clean old man." He'd never forgive or forget that one.

I sipped some onion soup and said as little as possible. A long day of hard knocks was catching up with me. For a time the combination of drugs gave me a sweet detachment; I was there but not there, watching these fascinating people with childlike awe:

Harry, a man my age who might be president; Linda, the most nearly perfect person I've ever known; and Amanda, who made bitchery an art form. I was honored to be in such exalted company, for I am, if the truth be known, a spectacularly dull fellow who spends his life coaxing words around and is clever, if at all, only in print, on the third or fourth draft.

Still, despite the brilliant company, by the time coffee arrived, I was starting to nod.

"Oh, look, Grady's going to pass out," Amanda said brightly. "Remember how he always passed out after dinner?"

I bared my teeth and said we'd better start home. Linda drove, and I played Sinatra's *Songs for Swinging Lovers* until I did indeed pass out. When we arrived, Linda helped me up the stairs, eased my clothes off, and examined my battered torso.

"Poor baby," she said. I flopped into bed, and soon she joined me. She turned out the light, and I put my arms around her and clung to her warmth as a man adrift in the ocean might cling to a life preserver.

"Can you make love?" she said.

Incredibly enough, I was wondering the same thing.

"It may kill me," I warned.

"Die happy," she suggested.

16

The next morning I was so sore I couldn't dress myself. From my knees to my neck I looked like a reject from Picasso's blue period. I crawled out of bed at noon, eased into a robe, opened a beer, and sent out an SOS to Elton Capps.

Elton arrived in twenty minutes, a big horse-faced Oklahoman in jeans and a fur-lined parka. He called himself a pig farmer these days, but there was more to his past than pigs.

Elton bought the farm next to us about six years ago. Soon people were warning me that my new neighbor was recently retired from the CIA and that he had been a legendary figure in that shadowy world, variously credited with (or blamed for) installing Marcos, ordering the execution of Ngo Dinh Diem, and plotting the overthrow of Allende.

An unsavory character, I thought, and kept my distance. In our first two years as neighbors we met only once, a brief handshake at somebody's crowded

141

Christmas party. Then, a few weeks later, during a snowstorm, I managed to get my Buick stuck in a ditch. I was sitting there cursing my luck when along came Elton Capps with a four-wheel-drive Bronco and a tow chain.

He freed me from the ditch with no wasted words, and I asked him over for a drink. Elton proved to be a serious student of both politics and bourbon. We disagreed on just about everything, but I liked him; that happens often in Washington.

He told me an interesting story that first day. He said he'd grown up on a ranch in Oklahoma not far from the state reform school. Every few months some boys would escape from the reform school, Elton said, and "my buddies and I would get on our horses and ride out there and chase 'em down like rabbits." I didn't think I could ever be on terms of perfect intimacy with a man who counted that story among his happy boyhood memories—to overthrow Allende was perhaps its logical conclusion—but we were friends nonetheless.

A few months later, Elton sought my advice. He'd written a book about his career as a spook, and two publishers had turned it down. I reluctantly agreed to read his hefty manuscript.

To my delight, Elton's manuscript was fascinating. It told me a lot more than I ever expected to know about the CIA and, in the process, even persuaded me that the agency might have some legitimate *raison d'être*.

I took Elton to New York for lunch with my agent, Fritz Hopper. Fritz doesn't read books—he says they give him migraines—but he sometimes listens to writers, and he loved Elton's tales of codes, coups, and counterspies. When Elton made a trip to the men's room, Fritz turned to me, his greedy little eyes aglow, and declared, "James Bond has written his memoirs!"

Fritz sent Elton's manuscript to a slightly disreputable publisher (the kind that makes gobs of money), dreamed up a jazzy title (*Superspook*), and when all the hardback and paperback and book club and foreign sales were tallied up, my friend the pig farmer had grossed three-quarters of a million dollars. (Fritz Hopper, of course, got $75,000 of that, and I got a free lunch.) There was a bit of a prepublication spat with the CIA, which threatened to take Elton to court, but all that did was sell more books.

I trusted and respected Elton. He'd played some dirty games, but I believed he had a code. There was much he wouldn't tell, but I thought he'd never lie to me. In the present mess, he seemed my best source of sensible advice.

I greeted him from the easy chair in my study and pointed him to the bar. He filled his glass, studied me a moment, and said, "What the hell is wrong?"

Amused, I pulled open my pajama shirt and gave

him a peek at my battered torso. "Jesus Christ," he muttered, and came and silently poked me over with long, skilled fingers. Satisfied, he said, "Who did it?"

I shrugged. "I don't know. Some hired thugs. Look, here's the bottom line. I need information about an Israeli who calls himself Uri. Mid-fifties, lean and fit, about six two, silver hair cut short . . ."

From the look on Elton's face I saw I'd made a connection. "A little scar on the point of his chin?"

I thought a minute. "Yeah, I'd forgotten."

"Maybe he told you his family fled Hitler?"

"That's him."

Elton put down his drink and leaned toward me. "His name is Rivka Elazar. Uri is a code name. He retired—it was all politics—as the number-two man in Massad, and he should have been number one. You've *met* this man?"

"Two nights ago, in Orth Butler's apartment in New York. It was the next morning, yesterday, I got beat up."

"Christ, Grady, what kind of a jam are you in?"

I told him the whole story. When I got to the part about the Arabs, Elton got up and went to the windows, first one, then another. He stood back from them, and to the side, so he could scan the outdoors without being seen. He didn't say a word—I kept on talking—but his instinct chilled me. As I continued the story, he kept gliding about the room, gazing out the windows.

144

Finally, I said, "That's all I know. I wish you'd tell me what the hell this Uri might be up to."

With a final glance outside, Elton sat down and gave me a long, unhappy look. "Jesus H. Christ, Grady," he said, and took a slug of Jim Beam.

"As far as his background—hell, you could write a book about the man. He's best known for directing the Mossad response to the Black September attacks on the Lod airport in May of '72 and at the Munich Olympics later that year. Do you remember them?"

I threw up my hands. "I was losing my first presidential campaign that year. Refresh my memory."

"An Air France plane landed at the Lod airport, outside Tel Aviv. At the baggage claim area, three Japanese terrorists produced automatic weapons and opened fire. Twenty-four innocent people killed, seventy-eight wounded.

"Massad began retaliation two days later. A Palestine leader's car exploded in Beirut. Six weeks later, another terrorist leader in Beirut opened a package and it exploded, blinding him."

"My God."

"That was only the beginning. It was much worse after the murder of the athletes in Munich. You can't imagine what a blow those two attacks were to Israel in general and Mossad in particular. It looked to all the world like they couldn't protect their own athletes, their own airport. Could the Palestinians isolate them, starve them out? They had to strike back, and Uri was the man they turned to. His goal was nothing less than to eliminate the entire leadership of Black September, wherever it might be.

"They didn't like going after PLO leaders in other countries because of the risk that their people could be captured and tried for murder. But they had no choice. First they gunned down a man named Zwaiter outside his apartment in Rome. Then Hamshari, Black September's man in Paris. They sent in a phony telephone repairman to his office, and when he answered his phone the next day, it exploded.

"The third target lived in the Olympic Hotel on Cyprus. He was reading in bed one night, and his room blew up. The next was an Iraqi professor who procured arms for Black September. He was gunned down in Paris, on the Rue Royale, not far from Maxim's. Twenty-four hours later, the replacement for the Cyprus operative—the one blown up in his hotel room—was blown up in *his* hotel room."

"That's enough," I said.

"It gets better." He had grown animated, like a baseball nut recalling the 1986 World Series. "It was brilliant; nothing in the history of counterterrorism can touch it. Uri's real masterpiece came in the Beirut raid in April of '73. The PLO leaders thought they were safe there, in their command posts, with armed guards; no way Mossad could reach them.

"Well, one night Uri sent in thirty-odd men. Some women, too, actually. Sent them in by raft, a few by

146

plane, dressed like tourists, hippies, young lovers—that's why he needed the women. Their objective was a seven-story apartment building, the PLO command post. The Israelis attacked in the middle of the night, killed the guards in the lobby, stormed the apartments of the PLO leaders, and gunned them down. They blew their safes and took records that were priceless.

"There was one unforgettable moment. The Palestinians upstairs realized there was a raid. They then made a serious mistake: They took the elevators down to respond. Uri and his men were waiting in the lobby. When the elevator doors opened, they simply shot the men inside, dragged their bodies out into the lobby, and sent the elevator back up for the next load.

"Finally they blew the building and left by helicopter. The entire operation took two hours. Two Israelis were killed, and more than a hundred terrorists and PLO leaders. The blow to the PLO morale, the boost to the Israeli morale—no price could be put on them."

Elton gazed out the windows again, then turned to me. "I want to impress on you that this is one of the most brilliant, most feared, most dangerous intelligence agents in the world. The fact that he's in America, personally directing a mission, means that something extraordinary is unfolding."

I blurted out something I'd held back. "He thinks there's a plot under way to attack—to destroy—Israel."

Elton nodded, as if that was understood. "I want to give you some advice. Get out of this thing. Whatever's happening, it's not your affair. You have no conception of the potential for violence involved. You're like a baby crawling across a minefield; you'd never know what hit you."

My aching body felt limp, rubbery. "The problem is my daughter," I began.

"Penny? Where is she?"

"At school. She's due home tonight, to spend the weekend."

"Good. Tomorrow morning, take her and Linda to Dulles and catch a plane, any plane. Fly standby. Be the last ones aboard. I'll come with you and make sure you're not followed. Fly to Miami or Phoenix or Los Angeles or whatever, then rent a car. Drive somewhere and spend a couple of weeks. Don't use credit cards or call anybody. Meanwhile, I'll be looking around. We'll arrange for you to call me on a secure line."

I shook my head wearily. "Penny will say she's got dates and exams, and Linda will say—"

"Dammit, man, we're not talking about exams. We're talking about people who would kill you and your wife and child quicker than you'd step on a bug! A little corner of hell just opened up, and you peeked in and saw things you weren't supposed to see, and they saw you, too! You're not safe here. Can't you understand?"

I stood up. "Okay, you're right. I'll do it."

My pig-farmer friend carried a rifle on a rack in the back window of his pickup. Before he left, he tucked his rifle under his arm and roamed around my property. He checked the barns and the woods down by the road. When he was satisfied, he waved and gave me his big toothy grin and drove off. When he was out of sight, I locked my front door for the first time since we bought the house; then I shivered and went around and locked the back door, too.

17

A cold rain washed away the last fading glories of autumn that afternoon. Out my window the black tree trunks glistened, and piles of gold and scarlet leaves lay in limp puddles beneath empty branches.

I took a long nap; it was dark when Penny woke me. We hugged, and I thought of the night when she woke me and told me John Lennon had been shot.

I have so many memories of Penny in those years. Once I got in a squabble with the White House. I had helped elect a president, and then I wrote a novel that he and his gang didn't like. When the book was published, reporters called and warned me that the next day's papers would quote various anonymous White House aides calling me seven kinds of a yellow dog.

I didn't care—lie down with dogs and you get up with fleas—but I was worried about the impact on Penny. I took her for a walk that afternoon and told her, "Sweetheart, the president is mad about my new book, and there'll be stories in the paper tomorrow calling me a lot of names. Don't pay any attention. They're a bunch of jerks."

Penny walked along, kicking a rock and thinking it over. "The president doesn't like your book?" she asked. She had met the gentleman, had suffered his toothy charm.

"That's right."

"Then he can go kiss a pig," she said.

Such was my baby at twelve; now she was a young woman, home from college, filled with enthusiasm and tales to tell. We joined Linda downstairs and sat before the fire, drinking beer and eating popcorn. Penny chattered about boys and fraternity parties and rock bands, told us about her work at the orphanage, and said she'd decided to skip sorority rush. "It's like they want to put you in their mold," she said. All that was fine with me; almost anything she wanted to do was fine with me.

I didn't mention her bounced checks and unpaid parking tickets or the midterm grades that had been almost as bad as mine used to be. I just wanted us to be happy tonight.

Eventually I went and poured a couple of beers into a pot and boiled some shrimp. We had that and salad and garlic bread for dinner; Penny had sworn off red meat and seemed to be flirting with Zen. After we'd eaten, I poked the fire and said, in a voice of pure reason, "There's something we need to discuss."

"What's that, Daddy?" asked my daughter.

"I talked to Elton Capps today about this damn thing with the Arabs. It's worse than any of us knew. Elton thinks we should go away for a while."

"Daddy, I've got *school*."

"We could work it out. How about a week in Florida? Maybe Key West, the Pier House. It shouldn't be crowded now, and—"

"You just want to stay there because the girls go topless," Penny said.

"What about our trip to France in June?" Linda asked.

"We can still do that."

"The Ryans are expecting us on Friday."

"Linda, for God's sake, our lives may be in danger. Look, the three of us haven't had a good vacation together since—"

"What about Bonnie?" Penny demanded. "We don't even know where she is! You just want to run away!"

So there we were. I fought against my temper. "Penny, I tried to find Bonnie and I couldn't. I got beat up, and Elton says there are people out there who'd kill us and never blink. Bonnie's father has private detectives looking for her. My job is to protect my family now."

"You could *try* to find her," Penny protested. "*I* could try!"

She was sitting on the floor by the fire. I knelt beside her, but she turned away. "Baby, I admire your loyalty, I really do. But it's too big for us. Her father's a senator. Her grandfather's a millionaire. They'll find her."

"No they won't!" she said bitterly.

I let her cry. Both of us, instinctively, were waiting for Linda to settle the issue one way or the other.

"I think we should do what Elton says," she said. "Maybe a week in Key West; then we could drive over to Naples. We could talk to Penny's dean if we have to."

I scrambled to my feet. "That's a great plan. We'll drive to Dulles in the morning and take the first flight. Let's all get some sleep now."

I wanted to close off debate before Penny counterattacked. Up the stairs I went, and soon the others followed. Florida it would be.

Linda and I sleep at the back of the house, and Penny's room is up front. That means she can stomp around or have guests or play her music or talk on the phone and we can still sleep. The next morning, when I looked back on it, I thought perhaps I'd half heard Penny on the phone when I was tossing and turning with my aches and pains, but that was nothing unusual; she'd spent the past five years making nocturnal calls to people all over the world. "Daddy, it's so cheap at night," she'd say, oblivious to the fact that it wasn't cheap if you talked two hours.

Linda and I were up early. "We'll just take one bag each," I insisted. Linda smiled sweetly; traveling light is not among her virtues.

I let Penny sleep as long as I could. She is dangerous when aroused. It was almost ten when I tapped cautiously at her door.

No answer.

I tapped a little harder.

Still no answer.

I screwed up my courage and looked in, aware that dirty words, a pillow, or even a shoe might be flung at me. The room was dark as a cave, and blankets rose like mountains atop her bed. I crept closer and finally realized there was no Penny beneath the blankets.

I ran to her bathroom. Empty. I shouted downstairs. No Penny. I stumbled back to her room, turned on the light, and saw the note on her pillow.

"Dear Mommy and Daddy: I have to help Bonnie. I think I can find her. Don't worry about me. I'm just a kid; nobody will pay any attention to me. You two go on to Florida and I'll call you next weekend when you're back. I love you both very much. Penny."

I looked out the window and saw that her car was gone. I let out a howl that shook the house. Linda came running up the stairs and found me sprawled on Penny's bed screaming, "Shit, shit, shit!"

She took the note and read it.

After a while she sighed and held my hand.

"You've got to go find her."

I ached all over, inside and out, body and soul; I felt a million years old. "I know," I said. "I know."

18

I was stumbling around, trying to pack, when Elton Capps called, thinking he was about to drive us to Dulles. I told him what had happened.

Elton cursed bitterly, then asked what time Penny had left. "I don't know," I admitted. "Probably before dawn. She could be in New York by now."

"Why? What the devil is she doing?"

"I didn't tell you everything. Penny knows the missing girl. They're friends. She's gone to find her."

He asked what kind of car Penny was driving and the license number. I told him. "What are you going to do?" I asked.

"I want a picture of her, too," he said.

"Come get one. They're all over the house. I may be gone when you get here."

"Where the hell are you going?"

"Where the hell do you think I'm going? To New York."

"I'll go with you."

His offer moved me. I was setting off on a one-man Pickett's charge, well aware of the dangers, and this man was ready to share them with me. Why? Not because I'd made him some money once. But because he cared about our family and because he lived by a code. I don't know many men like that. Yet despite my gratitude, and my fears, I knew what my answer must be. "No, I have to do this alone."

"You damn fool."

"I'll call you."

"Where are you going to stay?"

"I don't know."

"Don't tell anyone but me where you are. Dammit, Grady, don't trust anybody!"

"I won't," I promised.

"The phone call," he said. "Did Penny call the other girl or vice versa?"

"I have no idea."

"I'll check it," he said. "Call me—from a pay phone, collect—and I'll tell you what I find out."

I didn't ask how he would check. Once a spook, always a spook, I guessed. I muttered my thanks and hung up.

I packed one bag and tossed it in the backseat of my car. I put my gun on the front seat, under my raincoat. My body still ached from the beating I'd taken, and it wasn't going to happen again, not easily. It was still midmorning and I was ready to go, but there was one more call to make.

I had Harry's unlisted home number; he answered the phone himself.

"Penny talked to Bonnie last night," I told him. "Now she's gone. She left a note saying she was going to help Bonnie."

"Jesus Christ," Harry whispered. I guess he knew that Amanda's story about Bonnie's having a job was a lie.

"That's all I know. I'm going to look for them."

"Hold on, Grady. Don't go off half-cocked. We need to talk."

"There's nothing to talk about."

"We can help. Do you want to stay at Orth's apartment again? What can Lee Draper do? Do you have any leads?"

"No, I don't want to stay at Orth's," I said. "And I don't have any new leads. But this time it's my daughter, and that makes it different."

"Do they have friends from school they might stay with?" he persisted. "Bonnie always knew girls in New York she could visit."

"Yeah, Penny, too," I admitted. "I'll try to get some names."

"We could check their credit cards, too. Lee

Draper knows about things like that. And that call last night—Lee could check on it."

I didn't like the way Harry was moving in.

"Grady, I really appreciate what you're doing," he said.

More pretty words. I'd heard enough. "Yeah, well I've got to go."

"Where will you stay?"

"I don't know," I told him. "I'll call you."

I gave Linda a hug, fighting back tears, and drove up Route 15 through Maryland and Pennsylvania. I could reach Manhattan in four hours and not be at the mercy of the idiots who run the airlines.

It was a calm gray day, with a few patches of burnished gold still glistening on the hillsides, but all I could think of was Penny and the danger she was in. She'd always been that way. Headstrong, fearless. Horses were a big reason we moved to the country. Penny was winning ribbons before she could read. I hate horses; they're big and dumb and expensive and dangerous. Penny broke her arm jumping when she was six and didn't care; she kept riding with her arm in a cast. Thank God, when she noticed boys, she lost interest in horses. Boys are big and dumb, too, but all in all less dangerous than horses.

I passed Gettysburg, where I once interviewed Dwight Eisenhower not long before he died. You remember Ike. He's the one who warned us about the

159

military-industrial complex. I drove eighty and played old rock-and-roll tapes, trying to blast reality out of my head for a while.

I played a tape of rock classics I'd put together, one that started out with five consecutive versions of "Be-Bop-A-Lula"—by Gene Vincent, Jerry Lee Lewis, Carl Perkins, the Everly Brothers, and John Lennon. I played that once for Linda, rather proud of myself, and she said, "Are you trying to drive me crazy?" and threatened to leap out of the car if I did it again.

Mostly, on the way to New York, I tried not to think about what I'd do when I got there. How would I know until I did it? I longed for the Burma Shave signs of yesteryear—the first poem Penny ever learned was the immortal "Don't stick your elbow / Out too far / Or it may go home / In another car"—and for lack of their honest doggerel I studied the vanity plates on cars I passed. I saw a TACIT and a RANDOM and a GULP and a DO ME and a HOT UN. What the hell were these people trying to say? I read bumper stickers, too, although most of them were crude, the MINERS DO IT DEEPER sort. I passed two cars with SHIT HAPPENS stickers. Philosophers everywhere.

And so I drove north to find my daughter, not knowing what I would do, perhaps not perfectly sane, and not much caring anymore.

I checked into a big, anonymous Times Square hotel, then took a cab uptown to Monica's apartment house. The security guard on duty was middle-aged and dumpy. He said Buzz had quit and he had no idea where to find him. My guess was that Buzz was long gone, and I crossed him off my list.

I took a cab downtown to Annette's apartment. The guard said she'd moved and he didn't know where. He wouldn't let me inside to question other tenants, so I waited in a used record store across the street, watching through the window while I thumbed through their records.

A couple of hot dogs from a sidewalk vendor were my dinner. An attractive young woman came out of a Chinese restaurant and started up Bleecker Street. I ran to her and realized she wasn't Annette, but I fell in beside her, anyway. "Excuse me," I said, "but I'm looking for a—"

"Go away," she snapped without looking at me.

"It's important. Her name is—"

"Go away or I'll call a policeman!" It came out in one furious burst, and you had to respect her fear and anger. She disappeared around the corner, and I withdrew to a crowded neighborhood bar and ordered a beer. Some people were watching a tennis match. Two Czechs battling it out for $250,000 in Atlanta.

I asked the bartender about Annette, but he only shrugged. I finished my beer and took a cab back uptown to Ruth's brownstone. The door was opened by the man who'd been bartending on my last visit. I asked for Ruth, and in a moment she appeared behind him, as cool and elegant as always. "I'd like to talk to you," I said.

"No."

"It's important."

"Go away or I'll call the police," she said. The bartender slammed the door and locked it. I went to a doorway across the street. Rain was falling. Cars and taxis and limousines went by, honking their horns, sometimes stopping to let laughing, expensive people out, but no one came or went at Ruth's. I thought maybe I'd confront her at her office again, offer her money, threaten her, whatever. But tonight was a bust. I stood there in the rain, staring at her window, and finally caught a cab back to my hotel. I'd never felt so despondent, so helpless, in my life. Penny was somewhere in this accursed city, in danger, and I didn't know what to do.

I bought a bottle of Grand Marnier and took it up to my room. To ward off a cold. To focus my thoughts. To help me sleep. I have my drinking under perfect control. I only drink to excess at the worst possible moments.

I'd brought Penny's Madeira yearbook with me. I filled the bathroom glass with Grand Marnier and started calling the homes of girls from New York. I mostly reached parents, for the girls were off at college. I gave them some idiot story about Penny visiting a friend in New York and my forgetting her name. People were pretty nice, considering the hour. People who've shot $50,000 on the dubious blessing of a prep-school education tend to give aid and comfort to one another. I reached one girl who gave me the names of other friends of Penny's in Manhattan. By then I'd downed two glasses of Grand Marnier, and it must have shown, because a father told me curtly not to bother him "in your condition." I thought, *Brother, I hope you're never in my condition.* But if he had a daughter, he probably would be, sooner or later. Thus consoled, I drifted off to sleep.

19

The next morning was raw and cold. I sloshed to a noisy Broadway deli for coffee and juice, then called the number Uri had given me. Maybe I was counting on him to be my *deus ex machina*, the hero who'd unscramble this mess for me.

The number rang once, and a soft voice said, "Yes?"

"My name is Malloy. I want to get a message to Uri."

"What is your phone number?"

I hesitated. I didn't want to give out my whereabouts, even to Uri. "I . . . I can't be reached by phone. I'm moving around. Look, from noon till one I'll be having lunch at Orso's, on West Forty-sixth Street."

It was the first place that popped into my mind. But perhaps there was a reason: It was at Orso's that I'd had my first talk with Bonnie, and I had a gnawing, maddening sense that she'd said something I'd forgotten, something I needed urgently to remember.

After a moment's silence the person on the other end of the line hung up.

I called Sid Banks, the investigative reporter, and asked what he'd learned. "It was like I figured with your friend Nicky," he said. "He was supplying Monica with coke. Hung out at her place, too. Liked to sample the merchandise. His and hers both."

"What about Blair, the girl I told you about?"

"Nothing about her. *Nada.*"

"There's a lawyer I want to talk to, but I don't know his name. Early forties. Short, maybe five six, with reddish hair and fuzzy sideburns. A nasty-looking little guy. He won a big libel case not long ago."

"Kemper is his name. Bo Kemper. Where's he fit in?"

"I'm not sure yet. What about the cops? Any progress on the murders?"

"They're klutzing around, saying it was a drug deal. Except I hear there's interest from Washington."

"From who in Washington?"

"Haven't pinned it down yet."

"Okay," I said. "Talk to you later."

Ten minutes later I was in Bo Kemper's Park Avenue law office telling a very skeptical secretary I had to talk to him "about Annette."

While I waited, I thumbed through the current *People*. The magazine fascinates me. Who *are* all these people? Who *cares* who they are? Jesus, *I* was in there once.

Sooner than I expected, I was ushered into Kemper's office. If he was annoyed, he hid it well; he shook my hand, eased me into a comfortable leather chair, and asked in a whispery voice what he could do for me.

"I was at Ruth Orlando's place the other night. I saw that ape Allegro knock you down. If you intend to pursue it, if you need a witness, I'd like to help."

He made a steeple with his fingers and stared at me across the top of it, pondering my selfless offer. His blue eyes glittered with intelligence and malice.

"It was a personal matter, Mr. Malloy," he said softly. "I'll handle it my own way. Now, was that all you came to see me about?"

Kemper was wearing a flashy double-breasted, chocolate-colored suit. The little man was a dandy. I'd known lawyers like this before. They were killers, hired guns; they liked money and blood and big cars and young girls. I thought Annette, the preacher's daughter, was looking the wrong way for salvation.

"No, it's not all," I admitted. "I talked to Annette that night about a missing girl I'm looking for. I need to talk to her again, and I think you know where she is. I'd like for you to arrange a meeting."

Kemper pulled out a cigar and made a production

of lighting it. Finally, he said, "I read one of your books once, Mr. Malloy. The one about Texas. A hell of a yarn. Read it on the red-eye from L.A. and never put it down."

"I'm glad you liked it," I said humbly. We writers take our compliments where we find them; Tolstoy said the one reliable judge of art was a clean old peasant.

"So let me say, not wishing to appear rude, that even if I knew where Annette was, which I do not concede, it's quite impossible that I would put you in touch with her. Now, if that's all you had in mind . . ."

He rose from his chair. I did the same. "It's an urgent personal matter involving a young girl in trouble," I said. "I have no desire to embarrass you in any way."

His lip curled. "You're not going to embarrass me," he said gently. "Unless you put me in one of your books, in which case I'll sue you for all you've got and a little more. Good day, Mr. Malloy."

It was not a situation where you beg or plead or say, "Pretty please." You make your case, as one gentleman to another, and if the other gentleman turns you down you keep in mind the Kennedy maxim: Don't get mad, get even.

Down on the street, I called Sid Banks again. "That lawyer Kemper, is he a buddy of yours?"

"If Kemper was on fire, I wouldn't piss on him."

"He's keeping a girl named Annette who may know where Blair is. I just asked to see her, and he told me to get stuffed. You want to give it a shot?"

"You bet your ass."

"You want me to call you back?"

"Why don't you hold?" His tone was supremely nasty; Sid smelled blood.

I held. Jackhammers were blasting, and an irate matron was demanding the phone, but I hung on until Sid returned.

"Meet him in the lobby of his office building at seven. He'll take you to her."

"Jesus, what did you do to him?"

I hadn't expected an answer, but Sid said, "I told him I was doing an exposé of call girls and might use him and his chippy as Exhibit A."

Sid was the defendant in a libel suit. And Bo Kemper was a plaintiff's lawyer who'd just won a big libel case. Sid hated lawyers in general and plaintiffs' lawyers in particular and thus had focused a year's frustration on this brief encounter. Hell hath no fury like an investigative reporter sued.

I had some time before lunch, so I called more friends of Penny's who were in school in New York. They all sent their love to Penny, said they hoped to see her at the Christmas parties in Washington, and claimed ignorance of her whereabouts. After a while I walked over to Orso's.

Except for the pizza, the next hour was wasted.

I had hoped that if Uri didn't come he might at least send someone else, but no one came. I eyed the people in the restaurant, and some of them eyed me back, but not with the fate of Israel on their minds.

I was running out of ideas. I got out Bonnie's date book, made a list of the clients I could identify, and spent the afternoon going to their offices. A CPA was out of town. A lawyer wouldn't see me. A photographer burst into tears when he realized I wasn't a blackmailer. The only surprise came at the end of the day, when I talked my way into the office of an advertising executive whose name I had deciphered as Joe Drummond. There was some confusion with the receptionist. I didn't understand why she was giggling until she led me to a slender, fortyish, rather glamorous woman who was seated behind a long, tear-shaped desk.

"I wanted to see Joe Drummond," I said.

"I'm Jo Drummond," she said with a Modigliani smile. "What can I do for you?"

I didn't know what the hell to say. But her name and phone number *had* been in the date book.

We were in a bright, sleek office high above Madison Avenue, its walls covered with pictures of cosmetics and diet colas and bright Italian clothing.

"I . . . I'm looking for a young woman named Blair. She mentioned your name. I'm hoping you can help."

"Goodness. Are you a detective, Mr. Malloy?"

"No."

"I'm afraid I haven't talked with her in, oh, a month, and I haven't the faintest notion where she is."

"Yes, but perhaps she mentioned some friend or some place or some other lead I can follow."

Jo's face was fine boned and wary. She nibbled at her lower lip. "Is she in trouble?"

"I'm afraid so."

She sighed and stood up. "It's past five, Mr. Malloy, and it's been a horrid day. Have you ever dealt with Italians? Italian *men*? Perhaps we could have a drink."

She led the way to a small, quiet bar around the corner, a place with Tiffany lamps and polished wood and hunting scenes and bookshelves with real books. Most of the customers seemed to be stylish women like herself. We took a booth, and she ordered a Gibson and I, scotch. She ordered a glass of water, too, and tossed down a couple of Bufferin. "Those damned Italians," she muttered.

I still didn't know how Jo's name had gotten into Bonnie's notebook. "How well did you know Blair?" I asked with my world-renowned tact.

She downed half her drink in one graceful motion. "I'm really too tired to play games," she said. "Do you know about Blair's . . . *activities*?"

"Yes."

"You're not her father?"

"No, a friend."

She was silent for a moment. I waved to the waiter for another round. I'd had a hard day, too. "Blair is a sweet child," Jo said finally. "A sweet child who is temporarily lost, as people can be in our society, sometimes not temporarily. She's going through a period of rebellion. God knows I tried to reason with her, but she's deep into this sordid fantasy of hers, and she doesn't listen. She thinks she's discovering 'reality' and it's a thrilling adventure. Were you ever like that?"

"Sure, at about her age. And once I discovered reality, I decided that the real trick is to stay the hell away from it."

"Precisely." When she relaxed, she had a good, rather sardonic smile and canny eyes. "Blair has a talent for drawing, you know. I told her that if she'd go back to school I'd try to get her a part-time job at our agency."

"She can't take the cut in pay," I said bitterly.

"I suggested she live with me."

"Great," I muttered.

Jo cocked an eyebrow. "She could do worse."

I shrugged, not wanting to offend her, but it was too late. She finished her first Gibson, started on her second, and gave me a look. "Are you married, Mr. Malloy?"

"Sure." She could see my ring.

"I was married. Twice, in fact. I tried, truly I did. And I suppose that at some level I'll always like men.

I suppose, to be generous, that you can't help it that our culture reinforces your natural inclination toward boorishness and violence or that you blunder around in a state of perpetual heat or that you spend your lives in abysmal ignorance of what women truly want and need. I suppose you aren't entirely to blame for your mental and moral incapacities. I would even concede that you have endearing moments. Still, you can understand that an intelligent woman can very easily decide to live her life without you."

She knew I was a writer; perhaps that was why she was treating me to this manifesto. I wanted to beat a retreat, but part of me was fascinated. Only once before had I encountered such pure, unvarnished female hostility, and that was in a book, a little collection of graffiti from women's-room walls, the point of which seemed to be that all men deserved to have their balls hacked off with rusty knives.

"Are we really so bad?" I asked.

"Oh, in your own eyes, you're all princes. God's gift to the weaker sex. But the truth is that you hate us."

In vain did I protest that some of my best friends are women; she was hitting her stride. "Do you know what my second husband told me in a rare moment of candor? He said that whenever he read about a rape, part of him knew it was an outrage, but part of him was cheering for the rapist. 'Give it to her, brother!' were his precise words."

172

"You married him," I said. "We're not all like that."

"Aren't you? That's the question."

"Anyway, we do have to advance the species," I added.

"Oh, yes, I produced two fine children, did my bit for the species. And now, for the rest of my life, I'll live with someone who gives me pleasure, or I'll live alone."

Her eyes sparkled with self-satisfaction; she was enjoying this a lot more than I was. Unfortunately, like her ex-husband confronting rape, I was of two minds. If part of me wanted to pull out my caveman's club and bang some sense into her uppity head, part of me agreed that we men have a lot to answer for. If God's a woman, we're in deep shit.

"I once knew a very liberated woman who very much liked sex," I said. "She told me that sex with other women could be wonderful, but there came a point in the process when she wanted a stiff prick."

Jo's dark eyes smoldered. "When I want a stiff prick, I rent one. But all in all a vibrator is more satisfactory. And someone young and gentle like Blair is best of all."

She saw me wince. "Or does that offend your tender sensibilities?"

"She may be in danger," I said. "Don't you have any idea where she might be?"

Jo's face softened. Did I glimpse a flash of

173

maternal concern? "She was always very mysterious about her comings and goings. She kept changing apartments; it was all but impossible to find her. The only possible thing . . ."

"Yes?"

"It's so vague. She came to my apartment once very upset. More than upset, physically hurt. Something terrible had happened to her. I put her to bed and cared for her. She said some man, some drug dealer, had abused her, but she wouldn't give me the details or let me call the police."

"Nick Allegro," I said.

She nodded. "Yes, that was the name. She made him sound like a monster."

"That's what I've heard, too. I'm going to have to deal with him."

Her face, already flushed from the gin, turned nasty. "Deal with him?" she said bitterly. "Or cheer him on? 'Give it to her, brother!' "

Enough is enough is enough.

I lurched to my feet and glared at her. Part of me wanted to slug her or to throw what was left of my drink in her haughty face, but she would have liked that. So I only muttered, "Fuck you, sister," and stomped out of her posh little bar, leaving her there in the booth, a handsome woman in her forties, alone and half-drunk and, as far as I knew, happy as a clam.

20

Bo Kemper's law office was in a mile-high tower a few blocks north of Grand Central. Its lobby opened on both Park and Lexington and by seven was almost deserted. I shuttled between the two entrances, looking for Kemper, until a big pockmarked character in a black raincoat came out of nowhere. "Come on," he said.

I followed him onto Lexington. We stood in the cold rain until a black Mercedes shot to the curb. My escort jerked open the back door and said, "Get in."

He climbed in beside me. Kemper was at the wheel.

"Where's the girl?" I said.

"One more word and you're on the street," he snapped. I choked back a reply. The lawyer pulled into the traffic and made four or five turns before heading north on FDR Drive. He kept checking the rearview mirror, and the other one was twisted around, grimly studying the cars behind us.

"What about the Lincoln, Leo?" the lawyer said.

"Yeah," his sidekick muttered.

Kemper wheeled off the parkway at the last moment.

"He's still there," Leo said.

I was a passenger on the Paranoia Express. Kemper rounded a corner and hit the brakes. Leo rolled down his window and jerked out a gun. I froze, and all three of us watched as the Lincoln came around the corner. Somebody's blue-haired grandmother was at the wheel. Kemper cursed and started across town. Leo resumed his vigil of the rain-bright street behind us.

"You got people following us, Malloy?" Kemper muttered.

"You're out of your mind," I told him.

"Looks okay, Mr. Kemper." Leo was still fondling his gun. Mine was under the mattress in my hotel room. In theory, I wanted to go armed in this lunatic city, but when the moment came, I always backed down.

We were somewhere in the East Eighties. "Get down," Kemper barked.

"What the hell?" I protested.

"Down, dammit, get down!"

Leo gave me a shove, and I sat on my shoulder blades while we rounded a few more corners, then pulled into an underground parking garage. We took an elevator up, a long way up, to an apartment, a big, modish place, all blue and beige. The drapes were closed, I guess so I couldn't spot any landmarks. I couldn't understand all the cloak-and-dagger stuff; I just wanted to talk to Annette. Either Kemper didn't believe that, or he was scared to death of someone else. Nick Allegro was my best guess.

Kemper mixed himself a drink. "Want one?" he asked. *Beware of lawyers bearing drinks*, I thought, but I said, "Sure."

As he handed me my drink, Kemper asked, "You wired?"

"No."

Leo patted me down; then the lawyer nodded toward a closed door. "She's in there. You've got an hour."

I found Annette on a small blue sofa in a book-lined study. Gone was her "So Many Men" T-shirt. She sported white pants, a pink blouse, and an ugly bruise on her cheek. I shut the door. "You okay?"

She shrugged and held out her hand. After a moment, I realized she wanted my drink, and I gave it to her. "Sit down," she said. "I won't bite." She giggled, and I wondered what she was on.

I joined her on the sofa. "Is the room bugged?" I asked.

"Ask him," she said. "Probably not. You only care about Blair, and he doesn't care about her."

"What's he afraid of?"

"He said not to talk about him. Only about her. Jesus, what did you do to him?"

"The voice of sweet reason."

"Don't mess with him," she said. "Really."

"Look, you know what I want. I'm looking for Blair. I think she's still in the city, but I don't know where. Do you have any idea at all?"

Annette threw up her hands. Her brown hair was loose and radiant around her shoulders, but her face was profoundly sad. What could she fear so much that she would take this thuggish lawyer as a refuge?

"She could be anywhere. Uptown, downtown. She has lots of friends."

"Who would she turn to? Who did she trust?"

Annette laughed darkly. "Me. She trusted me. And Monica. Real winners."

She finished my drink for me. I decided to back up, to ease her into it. "Tell me how you met her."

"In a bar in the Village not long after she came to town. She was practically living in the street then, waiting tables and, you know, hanging out, but she was so damn pretty, and you could tell she had class. She just didn't give a hoot, you know? Guys, drugs, she was just so glad to be free of wherever she came from. I asked her to come stay with me, introduced her to Monica. I used to wonder about her, you know, background, but she never talked about it. Once she said her father was a lawyer somewhere down South."

There was a question I'd been meaning to ask her. "Did she ever use any name except Blair?"

Annette shook her head. "It was kind of a joke. She'd say Blair was enough."

"Are there bars where I might look for her?"

She named three or four Village clubs, but she added, "I don't think she'd go there if, you know, she was in hiding, because everybody sees everybody else in those places."

"People, Annette," I pleaded. "Who would she go to?"

She threw back her head in frustration. "God, there were so many people. I don't know everybody she knew. There was a girl in school in Virginia who was a real good friend—she called her a lot."

"I know about her. What about her . . . clients?"

She shrugged. "Clients aren't usually friends. There was an old movie director she liked; he was sort of like a grandfather. And she had a couple of dates with that big-shot editor, what's his name?"

"Giles Kessler."

"Yeah. And a CPA who invested her money for her. He had an Irish name."

"Invested her money?"

"Sure. Mine, too. He more or less guarantees you twenty percent; he's got this dynamite mutual fund. And there was a woman, an advertising executive, Blair liked. She went to her once when she was . . . sick. And there was that rock star, what's his name, they put him in the Hall of Fame? She went out with him sometimes."

"Annette, what about Nick Allegro?"

She shivered. "No, I won't talk about him. Anyway, he's not who she'd go to for help."

"I understand. But his name keeps coming up. What did he do to her?"

"It's not just her!" she cried. She turned away, hugging herself, trembling, then opened her purse and took out an antique pillbox and did some coke with a silver spoon so tiny it might have come from a doll's house. She offered some to me, but I shook my head. She smiled. "Coke's not so bad. It's the freebasing that messes people up." She breathed deeply two or three times. "Just since I've been in town, I've seen freebasing spread and change things, really waste people. That's Nicky's game, to get people freebasing, get them as messed up as he can, until he owns them."

I looked at my watch. "I talked to the advertising woman, Annette. I know Nick hurt Blair. Why?"

"Oh, God," she cried. "Listen, he's an evil man. He has physical power, and he has political power, too. The police won't touch him. Don't you know he's looking for Bonnie, too, just like you are? He thought I knew where she was, and he went to my apartment and beat my roommate, trying to find out where I was. Something about some tape she's supposed to have, I don't know. But I'm getting out, I've had enough, and she should, too. You think it's a huge city, but it's not. It's a small town, and if she's here, he'll find her."

It made no sense. Why would this cocaine dealer know about the tape? But Annette didn't know, and the minutes were ticking by.

"What did Nick do to her?" I asked.

She waited so long that I thought she wouldn't answer. "You've got to understand this crazy call-girl thing," she said finally, not looking at me. "The girls that a Monica or a Ruth is looking for, girls that men will pay five hundred dollars to sleep with, aren't girls off the street. They're girls with good backgrounds, with class, girls who come into it more or less for a lark. For the money, sure, but really they're slumming. Rebelling against their parents, whatever. It seems like such a joke at first, these fools who'll pay you five hundred dollars just for sex. It's like the joke about the girl who gave away a fortune before she figured out there was a market for it. You say okay, I'll do this a few times and then go to Europe, or back to school, whatever.

"Sometimes it works out fine. But sometimes it doesn't. Because it's not all harmless businessmen; the sharks are circling, the evil. Nicky, he's around; he'd hang out at Monica's and other houses, the big man with the mountain of coke. He's a smooth talker, a big spender, he's always saying, 'Hey, come over for a party.' And so many of them—of us—are so naive, we think we're smart, but we're total fools, and so

181

sometimes girls go to his place, and that's when—"

She choked up, buried her face in her hands. I looked at my watch again. "When what?"

She wouldn't look at me. "The thing you have to understand is, Nicky is half black, half Puerto Rican, he grew up in Harlem, he was tough and he was smart, and he fought his way up from nothing. He hates these rich girls, these college girls who come to town and think it's all a lark. He really *hates* them, wants to bring them down to his level. And he does. Oh, God, he does."

She fumbled in her purse for a cigarette. "Girls go to his apartment for a party; they don't understand that they're the party. He'll say some rock star is going to be there. Sometimes they are, but usually it's just him and his friends. Have some coke, honey. Hey, let's freebase, honey. I've seen them do it, seen how they drag it out because they know what's happening but the girl doesn't.

"It's party party party, whoopee, and then at dawn a girl's feeling pretty mellow and thinking what a swell time she's had and it's time to go. Then Nicky says, 'Hey, how about a quick one?' So she figures, *Okay, Nicky's a good friend to have, and I've probably snorted five hundred dollars' worth of coke, so fair's fair.* So she goes to bed with Nicky, and it's okay, and now the sun's up and she's ready to go home and sleep it off, and then one of his pals comes in. And then the next one. And the next one. Do you get the idea? Maybe the girl tries to fight back and gets slugged a couple of times and she starts to get the idea. Or maybe they freebase some more, to make it easier for her. After a while she doesn't know what's happening.

"Except she knows. Because they don't want just sex. They want to break her. Not with their fists—God, that'd be a million times better. They just keep on and on, three or four of them at a time. Things the girls've never done before—the things they wouldn't do for money because they were nice girls just having their nice sanitary thirty-minute dates with nice men like their fathers. Well, now they do those things, they do it all, maybe for two or three days, maybe with cameras, maybe with other girls, anything.

"Finally, the men get bored or have to leave, or whatever, and they let the girls go—call a cab and send them home. But they're not the same; they'll never be the same after that, inside or out, body or soul. Nicky crushed something inside them, their self-respect, I guess. Some go home after that, but some who thought they'd go home, or back to school, find out they can't go because they really are whores now, in their own minds, for the first time. To Nicky it's a big joke. The Initiation, he calls it, like a sorority. You get invited back again. And either you go or you leave town, that's the choice. You're in the club now; you get to watch the new girls brought in, the innocents, the . . ."—she started to sob again—"the virgins. Because that's what we all were before we went to Nicky's place, virgins, little girls playing games."

She took my hand and squeezed it, tears running down her face. My hour was almost up, and I was filled with hate, but I was no closer than ever to finding Bonnie and Penny.

"Where would she be, Annette? Where?" I was desperate, myself near tears of frustration and rage.

"I don't know; I swear I don't."

I tried to think, to remember, to force a deep-buried, festering fragment from my memory. "A boy-friend," I said. "Did she have some boyfriend?"

Her face was anguished, too. "I don't know. Yes, there was some boy."

"Who, please, who?"

"I don't know. Just a nice boy she met. She mentioned him once or twice. But it was like it was her secret, that she kept apart from her other life."

The door opened. Kemper was there, with Leo behind him. "Let's go, Malloy."

I turned back to Annette. "Give me a name, a place, anything!"

Leo grabbed my arm. I shook loose. "I can't remember," Annette sobbed. "I swear I can't." Leo grabbed me again. I started to hit him, but the whole thing seemed hopeless. I followed them into the front room.

"Give Mr. Malloy a ride home," Kemper said.

"Don't bother."

"We insist."

Leo and I took the elevator down. He nodded me into the back of the Mercedes. "Where to?" he growled.

"Times Square."

He started west in the light rain. I was thinking about Annette, Bonnie, that bastard Allegro, the elusive boyfriend. Then Leo swerved into an alley between two brownstones. It was dark as a cave. "Out," he said, and he was out first, waiting for me. I came out with my fists up, but he clubbed me on the side of the head, and I tumbled into some trash cans. He was coming at me, and I didn't have anything left.

Then a pair of headlights fixed us, blinded us. A car squealed to a stop behind the Mercedes, and we saw two men silhouetted, large men in raincoats. Leo faced them, snarling like an animal.

"He's got a gun," I said.

"Leave," one of them said to Leo.

Leo shot back an obscenity.

The man who had spoken moved more quickly than I would have believed possible. There was a crack of bone against flesh, and Leo was on his knees, whimpering like a baby.

The man took Leo's gun. "Leave," he said again, and Leo struggled to his feet and lurched away.

The other man followed him to the street. I could see better now. They were young, dark haired, familiar.

"Are you all right?"

"Yes. Who are you?"

"Go find a taxi. We will watch."

As I left, one of them was searching the Mercedes while the other watched the street. I got a look at their car, an old clunker, probably stolen and about to be abandoned. Where had I seen those efficient young men before?

Back at my cheap hotel I killed the Grand Marnier, watched a few minutes of Johnny Carson—he and his guests were jabbering in a language I did not understand—and soon fell mercifully asleep.

21

In the shower the next morning I realized Uri's young men must have been following me since I left Orso's. Nothing else made sense. I hoped they'd keep up the good work.

At breakfast an item in the *Times* caught my eye. Royce Knight was playing the Lone Star Cafe. I read that and grinned, and my thoughts went way back to the days when Royce and I had been friends in Nashville. He'd been the hottest thing in rock and roll for a couple of years, after Buddy Holly died and Elvis went into the army and Jerry Lee went into disgrace for marrying his cousin. Royce had three straight number-one hits, a season at the pinnacle, and then the Beatles arrived, and he couldn't give his records away. Royce had hard times then with drugs and ex-wives and record companies; for a dozen years he quit performing. Now he'd made a successful comeback. I wished I could see him, but there wasn't time, not on this trip.

187

Harry had given me Lee Draper's address in the West Sixties. I tried to call, but the line was busy, so I took a cab over. The rain had stopped, and the sky was an innocent blue. I got out at the corner and walked along Draper's street until I spotted his brownstone. Just then his door flew open and a woman hurried out.

To my amazement, it was Amanda; she almost knocked me down.

"Grady!" she cried. For an instant her cold little eyes narrowed; then she seized my arm and said, "I'm so glad to see you. We've got to find the girls. I was just talking to Mr. Draper. I think he can help, I really do. I must absolutely fly now. Meet me for lunch. At 21 at one?"

I mumbled my agreement; then a limousine slid around the corner, and she was gone. Amanda used to say she was born in a limousine and no one knew if it was a joke.

I knocked on Lee Draper's door twice before he came, looking surprised to see me. But he greeted me warmly and took me into a cozy library for coffee. He was wearing penny loafers, dark flannels, and a burgundy crewneck sweater, elegant as always.

"My home is my office," he explained. "A bachelor can do that, and of course the tax breaks are sensational. So, tell me what you've learned."

"Not a lot," I said. "What about you? Harry said you'd check the phone call to my house the other

188

night—when Bonnie called my daughter, or vice versa."

Draper sighed. "I checked it. The call was from a pay phone in Times Square. Which tells us nothing."

"How much do you know about Nick Allegro?"

He gave me a pained look. "How is he relevant?"

"Bonnie was involved with him. And I heard he was looking for her—looking for that damned cassette."

"That's impossible. Why would a drug dealer be involved in . . . in something like this?"

"I don't know," I said. "But he's a tough character. Maybe someone hired him to find it."

"He's not that tough," Draper said. "Dammit, Malloy, you don't realize what the stakes are here. That's why Orth and Harry are worried about you. Go home. Let professionals handle this."

"It's you who doesn't understand, Draper. My daughter is out there. I'm going to find her."

As we glared at each other, the phone rang. He seized it and muttered, "No, no, I'll have to ring you back." By then I'd cooled down. I might need this man. "What about Amanda?" I asked. "What is she doing up here?"

For the first time in our short acquaintance, Draper was speechless. "I saw her leaving," I explained. "Is she looking for the girls, too?"

"Yes, of course. She's calling friends of theirs,

looking for leads." He lowered his voice. "You understand, Harry would be upset if he knew she was involved."

"I won't breathe a word," I vowed. This was getting curiouser and curiouser. What *was* Amanda doing at Draper's place so early in the morning?

He stood up and extended his hand. "Don't worry, Grady, we'll find those girls," he declared. I returned his manly handshake, thinking I'd never disliked the son of a bitch more.

I went to a pay phone and dialed my home. Linda's first words were "Penny called last night."

"For Christ's sake, what did she say?"

"She's in New York. She said—and this is more or less a direct quote—'Tell Daddy I've got what he wants but there are other people looking for it, too. I'm with Bonnie and we're fine, but I need to talk to him.' I asked her where she was, or to give me her number, but she said she'd call back and I should get your number so she could call you."

I thought about that.

"Grady, for God's sake, give me your number!"

My fear was that somebody was tapping my home phone. Paranoia or realism? Either way it was an obsession with me. It was maddening: Penny and I were desperate to talk to each other, but we were both afraid to give out our phone numbers. I couldn't resolve the dilemma; I thought perhaps I'd talk to Elton, or perhaps Uri, and they'd have a solution. The thing was, Penny was safe, and I was terrified of doing anything that would make her less safe, that might send our unknown enemies racing to her before I could get there.

"Not yet," I told Linda. "I'll have to call you back. Didn't she say anything else?"

"No. Only . . ."

"Only what?"

"It was noisy. There were voices and music in the background. Like she was, I don't know, in a bus station or at a party or something."

That's my baby, I thought. *Half the killers in New York chasing her and she's found a party.*

"Can't you give me a number?" Linda asked. "What do I say if she calls back? Can't you see she's in danger?"

"I know that, Linda," I said wearily. "I'm trying to do what's safest. It's not simple."

"Okay. I'm sorry." A pause. "Elton wants you to call."

"Okay."

"Grady?"

"Yeah?"

"Are you okay?"

"I guess so."

"I'm afraid."

"Me, too."

"Be careful."

"Sure," I said.

I walked to another pay phone and called Elton's home but got his machine. Then I went to meet Amanda at 21.

I was on time, she was late—the story of my life. I ordered an old-fashioned, savored the day's first sweet kiss of alcohol, and soon found myself thinking about Harry and Amanda's improbable union, a classic example of opposites attracting.

You've heard about the politician who told the reporter, "No, I wasn't born in a log cabin. I was born in a manger"? Harry, in that great tradition, often reminds the voters of his humble origins in the Pacific Northwest, where his father owned a hardware store. What he didn't remind the voters was that he got the hell out of the Northwest and the hardware store at his earliest opportunity.

His athletic ability got him to Yale, his brains got him to Oxford, and then a malevolent twist of fate led him to meet Amanda in London. It goes without saying that they should never have married, but he was dazzled by her money, and she was dazzled by his good looks and brilliant prospects.

Amanda is essentially a decadent person. She has no interest in education or culture or public affairs— no interest in anything except the relentless pursuit of self-gratification. She should have married some suave, penniless Italian count—her money for his title, a fair swap, and no questions asked after that. But she married Harry, and they returned to Washington, where he had a Senate staff job, and then he did something quite strange.

At a time when millions of well-educated young Americans were pulling strings to stay out of Vietnam, Harry was pulling strings to get in, despite the furious objections of Amanda and her father, Orth Butler. Harry got his way, of course, and marched off to Marine Corps OCS, leaving Amanda behind, pregnant and bitter.

He came back two years later with a chestful of medals, a certified hero; that was when we met as neighbors in Cleveland Park. Harry and I shared an interest in tennis, spy novels, politics, and our young daughters, and despite our bitter disagreement over Vietnam, we became friends.

Amanda remained a problem, since she loathed Cleveland Park and didn't approve of scruffy types like me. She kept a full-time maid, her house always looked like something out of *House and Garden*, her dinners were excruciatingly formal—Amanda would tinkle a little silver bell, and her French maid would scurry in with the next course—and meanwhile, there we were next door, giving chili dinners where everybody sat on the floor, drinking Gallo and listening to my old Joe Turner albums. I think Harry secretly preferred our life-style, but he let Amanda have her way (she was, let us recall, paying the bills), and in time that meant moving from funky Cleveland Park to fashionable Spring Valley.

Amanda's mother was from Alabama, and she devoutly believed that child rearing was properly left to others. As a result, a lot of the nitty-gritty of raising Bonnie fell to Harry. The problem was that Harry's vision of parenthood was based on his Marine Corps experience: The officer lays down the law, and the recruit blindly obeys. As a result, our house became a refuge for Bonnie, a place where she could escape her parents, sneak cigarettes, listen to forbidden music, and otherwise be herself.

The question is how two people as mismatched as Harry and Amanda managed to stay married for twenty years. Part of it, I think, was social. The Kennedy years had made Washington fashionable, and Amanda, with her money, was a big fish in a small pond. She was up to her cute little ass in ambassadors who wanted to kiss her hand and solicit her money. And part of it was simply benign neglect. Politicians tend to ignore their wives, and Amanda didn't mind being ignored. She could amuse herself.

Finally, I think that at some point Amanda realized that Harry had a serious shot at being president of the United States, a prospect that at any given moment probably is keeping a quarter of the marriages in the Senate intact.

"Grady, you naughty boy, how many of those have you had?"

It was Amanda, arriving in a flurry, with the maître d' fussing over her. Did I neglect to mention

194

that since she had made the reservation, we had a choice table in the back room, that dark cave where Broadway producers and network presidents dine?

Amanda didn't apologize for being late; as far as she was concerned, the rest of the world had a silly habit of being early.

"We used to have my birthday parties here," she informed me. "Ice cream, cake, and champagne. When I was six or seven."

"You must have been the most popular kid on the block."

"We didn't live on a block—oh, you're being sarcastic, aren't you? Well, dammit, I *was* popular."

For a distraught mother, Amanda looked damn good. She was wearing a jade-green dress and emeralds, and she had a sly smile, a rosy glow; it occurred to me (burdened as I am with a dirty mind) that good sex could have caused that glow. Then I thought about that again, and it was no joke. Why the hell *had* she been leaving Lee Draper's place at ten in the morning? Could the elegant Draper be making whoopee with the boss's wife? I knew he was a fool, but was he that great a fool?

"Grady, I'm sorry about what I said to you the other night. You *were* terrible not to tell us about Bonnie, but I still shouldn't have spoken so strongly to an old friend."

"You were eloquent, Amanda. I was honored to be the object of such passion."

195

"Oh, Grady, you'll never change."

She favored me with a lingering smile. It wasn't precisely an I-want-to-screw-you smile—the hair-trigger recognition of which can be vital to a man's happiness—but it was clearly an I-want-something smile. But what did she want? And what about that apology? Amanda had always lived by the never-apologize, never-explain rule.

We ordered lavishly—*something* had given her an appetite—and she pumped me about what I'd learned. I decided to be honest, within reason. "Amanda, I just had a message from Penny. She said she and Bonnie are okay."

"Where are they?" she asked quickly.

"She didn't say; she's going to call me."

Amanda gripped my arm. "I want you to give Bonnie an urgent message. Tell her I'm at the Pierre and she must come there at once, to my room—if I'm not there wait for me, with the door locked. She isn't to speak to her father or grandfather; she's to come to me at once. Do you understand?"

I understood the message but not what lay behind it.

"What is it, Amanda? What are you afraid of?"

Her cat's eyes burned with sudden passion. "You don't understand anything, do you, Grady? Not anything."

We were drinking champagne, drinking it rather fast. We finished the bottle, and I called for wine.

"You've always thought I was a terrible mother—no, don't deny it—and maybe I was. But I love my daughter. She's the most important thing in the world to me. I won't let them destroy her."

"Let who destroy her, Amanda?"

Our entrées had arrived, and instead of answering, she attacked her steak tartare fiercely, as if she were devouring her nameless enemies. When she had finished, she pushed her plate away and fumbled in her purse for a cigarette. I lit it for her. She inhaled angrily, held it, and sent smoke cascading above my head. I waited.

"My father wanted to be president," she said abruptly. "For twenty years he imagined that they'd turn to him, draft him. It was insane, of course—my God, the skeletons in that man's closet—but he believed it."

When she didn't continue, I said, "It's a popular fantasy, Amanda. At any given moment, half the cabinet, half the Senate, and countless generals and corporate executives and football coaches and college presidents and movie stars share it. They never notice how hard the people who get there have worked to get there."

"Daddy's no fool," she said. "He finally realized it wouldn't happen, and then he decided to elect Harry."

"He'd be a good man to have in your corner," I said.

"Damn you, Grady Malloy, listen to me. This isn't chitchat. My father is obsessed. He's determined to put Harry in the White House. He won't let anything stand in his way. He'll lie, he'll cheat, he'll kill . . ."

Your typical campaign manager, I thought, but I decided I'd better take her seriously, that she was trying to tell me something even if she wouldn't quite come out with it.

"The Arabs," I said. "What does all this have to do with the Arabs?"

She shut her eyes again; she seemed to be holding her breath, summoning all her strength. "Get that damned cassette," she whispered. "Get it and give it to my father and promise him you'll never speak another word about it."

I thought that she was trying to tell me something, that despite our mutual distrust we were somehow allies. "What's on the thing, Amanda?" I pressed.

"It doesn't matter what's on it! Can't you understand that?" She spoke so loudly that people looked around. She caught herself and smiled sweetly. "I've got to go now, Grady. You can see me to a cab— Don't worry about the check; it's taken care of. You were sweet to come."

The moment was past; Amanda had told me all she was going to tell me. Outside, while her limo blocked traffic, she took my hand, oblivious to dozens of honking horns. "One other thing, Grady. Promise me you won't mention my meeting with Mr. Draper. Harry wouldn't approve of my meddling."

"I promise, Amanda," I said. And then I added, "Do you trust Draper?"

Her eyes were cold and perhaps slightly amused. "Well, he does work for us," she said, and then she was gone.

I walked back to my hotel. I'd learned something at lunch, but I wasn't sure what. I was halfway convinced that she was sleeping with Draper and I'd blundered into her exit that morning. Part of the purpose of lunch was to win my vow of silence. But what about the rest of it? Her vague but impassioned warnings against her husband and father? Was that for real or only window dressing, a show she put on to dazzle and divert me? I had no idea. Amanda was a big-league liar, a DiMaggio of duplicity, and a bush leaguer like me could go crazy trying to second-guess her.

Back in Times Square I called Elton collect. This time he answered. "Is your phone okay?" I asked.

"Yes," he said tersely. "What's happening?"

I told him the highlights—about Penny's call, the guys who saved me from being beaten, my talk with Draper, and Amanda's vague warnings. Elton grunted a few times but didn't say anything. Finally, I gave him the name and number of my hotel. "Give that to Linda," I said. "She or Penny can call me there. But if Penny calls and I'm not here, you should call her immediately—tell her a place to go until I can meet her. Okay?"

"Yes," Elton said gravely. "Grady, I'm going to your house so Linda won't be alone and so I'll be there if Penny calls. All right?"

"Of course."

"One other thing. That call, the night Penny left. It was made from a pay phone in Greenwich Village."

"The Village? Are you sure?"

"Absolutely. Why?"

"Lee Draper, Harry's man, told me it was placed from Times Square."

"He's lying," Elton said. "Watch out for him."

"I will," I promised.

22

I spent the afternoon in my hotel room, hoping Penny would call. But she didn't, and in the evening I ventured out, checking back with the hotel switchboard every half hour or so. I visited some of the bars Penny's friends had mentioned, but the bartenders laughed at my inquiries; they saw thousands of sweet young things every week, as interchangeable as daffodils.

Bonnie and Penny were somewhere in New York, but I didn't know where. I thought I'd go crazy if I just waited for Penny to call. I felt better out looking, doing something. Then, somewhere in the battered recesses of my brain, I made a connection. Annette had said Bonnie had gone out with a rock and roller, one who was in the Hall of Fame. That narrowed the list to a dozen or so, and one of them was my friend Royce Knight. So I went to the Lone Star Cafe that evening for a journey to the past.

I arrived for the second show and found a table on the balcony, overlooking the bandstand. I ordered

201

a burger and a beer; then Royce came onstage, and I laughed with joy and was carried back to Nashville, twenty-odd years before, to the days when I wrote a country-music column for the *Tennessean*. One night I was having a beer at Tootsie's Orchid Grill with a music publisher named Buddy Killen. Buddy pointed to a kid hunched over the pinball machine. "See that boy? He could be the next Elvis."

I saw a skinny youth in boots and jeans and duck-tails; he could have been any of a thousand young guitar pluckers lusting to be the next Elvis. But there was something special about this boy, his intensity, his sleek, perfect profile, and I asked Buddy to invite him over. The three of us ended up back at my apartment, where Royce sang us his songs until dawn. When he cut loose with "Tornado," Buddy winked at me and whispered, "Number one!"

A week later they recorded "Tornado," and two months later it *was* number one. In the meantime, I'd written a column about Royce, and he appreciated it—most reporters were still making fun of rock and roll in those days—and that summer, after he'd had his second hit and been on Ed Sullivan's show, I went with him on a tour. It was the damnedest thing I ever saw, at least until my first presidential campaign. Wall-to-wall teenyboppers beating down doors, climbing in windows, bribing bellhops, doing any-thing to get their hot little hands on Royce—or me or his drummer or his bus driver or anyone who even faintly reflected his glory. Royce didn't neglect the little girls, but his music came first; at some point he would lock his door and take out his pencil and pad and write songs. I remember him telling me, "Those kids, they inspire me; I don't care so much about the screwin', Grady, but I've got to *understand* 'em, 'cause that's all I've got."

For about two years Royce did understand them as well as anyone; he was plugged into the kids' wavelength, perfectly attuned to the dreams and heartbreaks of teenage America, and he wrote two or three songs that will live as long as "Cathy's Clown" or "Runaround Sue" or "Sweet Little Sixteen," as long as people listen to rock and roll. But then his records stopped selling, and he got into drugs and fights with his record company and all the rest of it. One day in 1970 a guy called me and said Royce was being held in a private mental institution. His third wife had had him committed—she said he'd tried to kill her—and he'd bribed a guard to call me. I hired a lawyer and won his freedom, but then Linda and I left for a year in France, and I lost touch with Royce. I read in *Rolling Stone* that he'd given up performing and returned to his family's farm in West Texas, and then, about a year ago, I read about his sold-out comeback engagement in Las Vegas.

Now, from my balcony, I saw him emerge from the shadows, grinning, confident, a prince of rock and roll in his old faded jeans and dusty boots, and all my affection for him welled up. When he hit the opening chords of "Tornado," my eyes burned. Royce was a lot of things, but down deep he was a dreamer from West Texas who'd never wanted anything except to make his music; he'd paid a high price for his dream, but he'd survived, still making music, and some of us would always love him.

When he finished his set, I went down to greet him.

"How ya doing, pal?" I grinned.

He stared at me a moment. Royce's face was rounder now—he wasn't pretty anymore—and there was a wary toughness to it, but then he grinned back, and I saw the boyish innocence that was the wellspring of his genius. "Grady, son of a gun, is it really you?"

We embraced, pounding each other on the back, and he led me over to his table.

"How the heck you been?" he demanded. "I read all your books. You're really grinding 'em out."

"Doin' my best," I said.

"You'n me, Grady, we're artists, we live by our wits."

"I hear the comeback's a big success. They even put you in the Hall of Fame."

Royce made a face. "I should have gone in the first year. The damn record companies—they've got it rigged."

The waiter brought him a cup of coffee. He emptied two sacks of sugar into it and began to stir. "You off the other stuff, Roy?" I asked.

He shrugged. "A little wine, a little weed, but nothing heavy. Once I licked speed, I stayed clean."

He sipped his coffee. "You remember one time, Grady, I said when I was forty, if I lived that long, I didn't want to be singing 'Tornado' and 'Eddylou'?"

"Sure I remember. I put it in my column."

"Well, I am singin' 'em. 'Cause that's what people want. I'm writing new stuff that's better, but they want the old stuff. So here I am. Singing 'Tornado.' A fuckin' oldie but goodie."

"People love it, Royce. It makes us young again."

I meant it. When I heard Royce's songs, I was a kid again, courting Linda, dancing in the Tennessee moonlight, younger than my daughter's generation would ever be.

Royce smiled wistfully. People had started to gather around, wanting his autograph or talking about the old days. A chunky woman in her forties hugged Royce and giggled about "that night in Buffalo" and introduced her daughter, who giggled, too. Royce gulped and mumbled and soon told me, "Come on, let's get out of here." He slipped on a leather jacket and led me out onto Thirteenth Street. His drummer and bass player trailed along behind us.

"Tell us about that night in Buffalo, Royce," I quipped.

"Man, sometimes they point to their kids and wink, like . . . you know. Or some good-looking girl will come up and say, 'I think you're my daddy.' " He sighed. "I could tell you some stories, pal—give you a *real* book. Hey, how about a drink?"

"Sure," I said. "Where? The Village?"

"I know this guy, he's probably got a party going at his place uptown. Let's check it out."

"Sure," I said. "Who is he?"

He waved for a cab. "Oh, sort of a businessman. A real character. Deals a little dope."

Royce could be maddeningly vague. "What's his name?" I pressed.

A cab stopped for us. "Huh? Oh, his name's Nick. Nicky Allegro."

I had only a moment to decide. I wanted to see Allegro's apartment. I half expected to find Bonnie there, or someone who knew where she was. Was it safe to go there? As far as I knew, Allegro didn't know me. I feared Allegro, but he seemed to be the spider at the center of the vast web I was in. I was desperate. I kept wondering why Penny hadn't called me, fearing she was a prisoner somewhere.

"Sounds great," I told Royce. "Let's do it."

He gave the driver an address far uptown. The drummer and bass player climbed in, too, but they had their own conversation going, something about religion, and they were oblivious to Royce and me. I told Royce I'd been looking for a girl named Blair who'd said she knew him. He thought a minute. There'd been so many women in Royce's life; he could barely keep his ex-wives straight. "A tall blonde? Real pretty but kinda moody? Kinda drifts in and out?"

"That's her."

"I met her up at Nicky's, took her out a couple of times. See, when I go to these openings and clubs, I need a foxy chick on my arm. Gotta keep up the image."

"Do you know where she lives? Do you have a phone number or anything?"

He shook his head. "She always came to my place. Hey, you want me to ask Nicky? He might know."

I thought a moment. "Yeah, ask him. But don't tell him I asked. And don't tell him my name. Tell him . . . hell, say I'm your lawyer from Nashville."

Royce shrugged; he was a past master at this sort of intrigue. On his tours, he'd have three or four women he was juggling, on different floors of his hotel. To change the subject, I asked, "You're not involved with anybody?"

"I'm off women," Royce said. "Man, they suck your blood. I pay fifty thousand a year to wives I can't remember and kids I've never seen. If I want a date, I call an escort service."

"You don't mean you're celibate, Royce?"

"Naw, man, but I done quit screwin'!"

We had a good laugh on that. Royce liked to play

the hillbilly, but he was in some ways a highly sophisticated man. I was forever fascinated by his mix-
ture of toughness and vulnerability. There was
something eternally childlike about Royce; women
had spoiled him, and stardom had isolated him; he
was a kind of gorgeous monster, a beautiful, brilliant,
innocent, spoiled child, following his star and never
paying much attention to the people he devoured
along the way. I knew a couple of those women he
remembered as bloodsuckers; they had bittersweet
memories of Royce as a beautiful boy who fell madly
in love with them, wrote songs about them, then
drifted away when they had babies. Maybe that was
Royce's curse, the price he paid for his talent, to be
condemned to fall in love, over and over, forever.

"How many times have you been married,
Royce?"

"Five, I think. A couple were annulled—you
don't count those, do you? The women I really loved
I never married; it would just have spoiled it. The girl
I wrote 'Eddylou' for—she's married to some damn
dentist in Abilene now." He sighed. "You still with
Linda?"

"Twenty-two years now," I said.

He shook his head at the wonder of it. We were
shooting up Madison Avenue now. "You mess around
any?"

I laughed roguishly. "Royce, as a matter of fact,
Linda doesn't know I'm up here—it's kind of com-

plicated—so at this party, for God's sake don't use my real name. Call me something else. Call me . . ."

Royce grinned, pleased to find me among the fallen. "Hey, I'll call you Melvin T. Stubblefield!" He roared, recalling a demented hillbilly songwriter we'd known in Nashville. "Hey, guys, meet Melvin T. Stubblefield."

His two musicians glanced at us as if we were mad, and soon our taxi stopped at the apartment tower on 110th Street where Nick Allegro lived.

23

In the lobby a young couple was talking to the security guard, a Latin in a too tight gray uniform. Two more Latins in gaudy sport shirts were lounging nearby.

The boy was your basic assembly-line preppy in a blue blazer and regimental tie. He was handsome, obnoxious, and drunk. "Look, my man, just tell Nicky it's Frazier Holloway, met him at Club 97 last week, told me to come by anytime."

"Frazier, it's late," the girl whispered as the guard called upstairs.

While we waited, I found a pay phone in the corner of the lobby and called my hotel, but there still was no message from Penny.

The girl with the drunk preppy was about nineteen, big-boned and soft, with a hint of baby fat about her cheeks and arms and hips and a sweet, pale face, with rosy cheeks and wide, myopic eyes. She wore a polo coat over a plaid skirt and fuzzy pink sweater, and she didn't look as if she belonged with the surly Frazier or anywhere near 110th Street.

"College kid, says he met you, got a girl with him," the guard muttered into the phone.

"Lemme talk to him," the boy said, and grabbed the phone. "Nicky, dammit, j'ya invite me over or not?"

He listened a moment, then glared at the guard triumphantly. "He says to come right up!"

The guard spoke into the phone in Spanish, then nodded toward the elevator. "Top floor."

The boy took the girl's arm and pulled her toward the elevator. She held back, uncertain, but he was hotdogging now, the man about town, the friend of coke dealers and Harlem gangsters. I looked at the two guys in the chairs, maybe the two who'd beat me up, but they weren't paying any attention to me now. They were eyeing the girl like wolves who'd spotted a plump little lamb. One of them made a kissing sound as she passed.

"Hey, Mr. Knight, welcome back," the guard said to Royce. "How was the show?"

"Good show," Royce said. "These New York audiences, they're real alert."

"These guys with you?"

"Yeah, three shitkickers from Nashville."

"Go on up. Nicky's there, bunch a people there."

We shared the elevator with the young couple. The boy eyed us disdainfully, as if we were crashing

211

his party, but the girl blushed and said, "Mr. Knight, I really love your music. My mom does, too. My name's Deena, Deena Cole."

Royce gave her a wink. I think talking to him made her feel better. She knew she should go home, but she couldn't convince her idiot date, and she didn't have the gumption to strike out on her own. I bit my lip and said nothing. I had my own problems, like what I would do if Allegro or his henchmen recognized me.

The elevator opened onto a hallway, a desk, another Latin with a shoulder holster. He grinned at the girl and hit a buzzer. The inner door opened, and suddenly Allegro filled it, his beard glistening, his eyes hard and black. He looked like what Pavarotti would look like if Pavarotti was twice as big and a psychopath.

The boy blundered on, hand outstretched. "Nick, Frazier Holloway, met'cha las' week. This is Deena."

Allegro's hand swallowed up the boy's. "Good of you to come," he purred. He turned to the girl, bowing a little. "Such a pleasure," he said. "Come in, miss. You see anything you want, it's yours."

The girl squeaked a hello, awed by his mountainous presence, and then Allegro turned to us. "Royce, you crazy fuck, where you been? I got a new toy to show you."

"I brought some of the guys," Royce said. Allegro

grunted in our direction, clearly uninterested in Royce's entourage.

He led us into a big, dark room that was somewhere between a warehouse and a nightclub. Furniture was scattered around at random, and dirty dishes and bottles and potted plants and people huddled in tight little groups. There was a bar, some spotlights, throbbing disco music, and at one end of the room a semicircular platform or dais with three steps leading up to it and a wrought-iron railing around it.

Allegro led us to his new toy, a classic forties Wurlitzer jukebox. "Mint condition," he boasted. "Got all your stuff on it. Listen." He punched some buttons, and "Eddylou" came wailing out.

"Hey, cool," the preppy said, and grabbed the girl's hand. They danced a few steps, but her heart wasn't in it.

"You boys get yourselves something to drink," Allegro told me and the musicians, and he led Royce and the young couple up to the dais, the throne from which he could survey his domain. The musicians and I—Mick and Terry were their names—grabbed a beer and claimed three folding chairs in a dark corner. They kept arguing about religion—Terry, it developed, was a born-again Christian; Mick, a belligerent atheist— and I studied the big, dark room.

Up on the dais, Nicky was introducing Royce to half a dozen honored guests. I recognized a comedian

I'd seen on the Letterman show, a famous fashion model, and one of the NFL's all-time great running backs. They clustered around Royce, grinning and hugging him, and he accepted their homage as his due.

The only one who wasn't grinning was a slender Latin who sported ratty sideburns along with a tan suit and a chartreuse shirt. He stood stiffly, his hooded eyes darting between Allegro and Deena.

From where I sat, what came next was acted out in pantomime, but it wasn't hard to understand. The preppy was trying to get a few words in, to be a big man, but Allegro wanted no part of him. Allegro locked one arm around the young couple and the other around the guy in the chartreuse shirt and sent the kids off with the sidekick.

The preppy wasn't happy at being dismissed, but the sidekick was sweet-talking him, leading him to a table by the jukebox, and when he tossed some coke onto the table, Frazier Holloway brightened up considerably. The girl was cringing beside the boy, pleading with him, but she had lost him to the thrilling prospect of free cocaine. Some other Latins glided over, forming a circle around the young couple, but Frazier Holloway just gave them a cheery wave and started snorting.

Mick was out of cigarettes and clomped up to the dais to bum some from Royce. When he returned, Terry said, "What's happening up there?"

Mick giggled. "Girl just asked Royce how he liked Elvis."

We all had a laugh on that. Royce hated Elvis, hated his music, hated his looks, even hated him for dying because it sold more of his records.

"And Royce is telling war stories," Mick added. "You know, Vegas, how he wrote 'Eddylou,' thrilling tales of yesteryear."

I had to smile. I'd heard all those stories—the tales of the girls he should have married but didn't and those he shouldn't have married but did, tales of week-long orgies with Vegas showgirls, tales of touring with Chuck Berry and Bo Diddley in the golden years. Royce was enjoying himself—being lionized, being a star; that was his life, what he had instead of a family and a home—and I was down in the shadows trying to decide what to do next.

I had wormed my way into Allegro's stronghold, but now that I was there, I didn't know what to do. People were tightly clustered, punk rockers here, Latins there, Broadway types somewhere else, and to bang around asking questions looked like suicide.

The place was noisy, confused. Mick and Terry were sharing a joint and arguing about Jesus, some punks were draped over the jukebox, some blacks and Latins had a card game going, and all the while I was keeping my eye on Deena, across the room. The Latin in the chartreuse shirt—Raul, Mick said his name

215

was—was a smooth little man with a hairline mustache and dainty hands that never stopped fluttering. He filled her glass, rolled a joint, laid out lines of coke, all the time keeping up the patter.

Frazier Holloway thought he'd died and gone to preppy heaven: guest of honor in a coke dealer's lair, being served up free dope, a stash as big as the Ritz. What a tale to take back to the Kappa Sig house. He passed a joint to the girl and persisted until she took a hit. She sipped her wine while the boy did four lines of coke; then he started after her to take some. I could imagine his argument: Don't be a jerk; it's free.

Up on the dais, someone had brought Royce a guitar, and he was clowning his way through "Heartbreak Hotel." The model was coming on strong to him; I wondered if she could penetrate his hard-won misogyny. I remembered once when he was living with a plain woman named Zena and he told me scornfully, "What's beauty? Nothing but skin, skin, and bones." That's the philosophy of a man who's slept with more beautiful women in a good weekend than most of us have in our whole lives.

Deena did some coke. You could see her start to relax, to go with the flow. The preppy was wired, talking a mile a minute. Raul spoke to a Latin girl, and she stood up, sullen, unsmiling, and left the room. I got up, too.

"Where ya goin', man?" Terry asked. He had long hair and a beatific look.

"To pee."

Mick said, "Careful, it's a jungle out there," and giggled.

I walked over to two black-clad punks, one with pink hair and one with blue. They were arguing about where Elvis Costello had gotten his name. I said, "Say, do you fellows know a girl named Blair?" The one with pink hair looked at me, then at his friend, then started talking about Elvis Costello again.

I found the kitchen, and it was a wreck: empty bottles everywhere and dozens of bulging trash bags waiting for somebody to haul them away. The Latin girl was at the stove waiting for water to boil. Freebasing, it's called; you cook the coke until it turns to crystals, and you smoke it and get one hell of a rush.

"Whatta you want?" she asked. She was a sweet little handful in designer jeans, spike heels, and a silk blouse; ninety-five pounds, maybe, and twelve kinds of trouble.

"Do you know a girl named Blair?"

"Fuck off, asshole."

I never argue with a lady. I found a phone and called my hotel, but there still was no message, so I returned to the party. Raul had Deena dancing now, twirling her around, ballroom style. The other Latins and their women just sat on the sofas like vultures.

Allegro had taken a call at the bar. Not far from him, the two punks' argument had escalated. The one with blue hair pushed the other one and yelled, "You bitch!"

Allegro moved gracefully for such a big man. He chopped the pink-haired boy with the side of his hand and did something terrible to his nose. It spurted blood, and the boy howled in pain. "Get him out of here," Allegro muttered, and the other boy helped his battered friend out of the room. The attack had been entirely unnecessary; the boys weren't causing any trouble. The son of a bitch just enjoyed it.

"That dude don't mess around," Mick said.

"How late you guys gonna stay?" I asked.

"Beats the 'Late Show,' " Terry said.

Royce walked to the jukebox and punched some buttons. I joined him. "You ask him about Blair?" I said.

"Yeah, he said he thought she'd left town." Royce didn't seem much interested in me; probably his mind was on the model. To be Royce's friend you have to understand he has a short attention span; we get along because we only see each other every four or five years.

He rejoined the model, and I retreated to my dark corner. Raul had the two kids freebasing, the boy eagerly, Deena in a daze. I doubted if she knew where she was anymore.

The boy passed out. Raul had his arm around Deena, laughing, keeping her on her feet, giving her more wine. He started rubbing her bottom, and she

218

didn't seem to notice. Her eyes were half-closed. He winked to his friends and guided her toward a door that led to the bedrooms.

"You see that?" Terry asked.

"Cherry pop," Mick muttered.

I cursed under my breath. But what the hell could I do?

I glanced at Royce. The model was wrapped around him, and you could see him starting to melt. Poor Royce. After two decades of disaster he still believed in true love. Deena probably believed in it, too; she'd have a lot to think about tomorrow. She'd wake up feeling awful, remembering little, but knowing something terrible had happened. She wouldn't know what to do, and Holloway would tell her to keep her mouth shut lest he get in trouble, and she would, because she was the kind to suffer in silence. For a long time.

For an instant I hungered for that wonderful detachment that drugs can bring, so I could look around this big, ugly room, with its tableau of lust and greed and hate, and not give a damn, not feel responsible, be only bemused by the pointlessness of it all.

But I wasn't detached. I was angry, half-crazy. The jukebox was playing The Eagles' "Hotel California." I remembered hearing it in Paris in the summer of 1978 while I was eating ice cream with Penny in a little Left Bank café. Where the hell was she now?

I wished I had a bomb and could blow this room to hell. I remembered all kinds of crazy sentimental crap; then I got up and headed for the kitchen.

No one was there. The back wall was more or less covered by a mountain of bulging trash bags. There was a door behind the pile. I unlocked it and saw that it led to a service elevator. I left the door unlocked and tore open one of the trash bags. It was filled with beer cans and the remains of TV dinners and Spanish-language newspapers. I set fire to some newspapers and got the hell out.

I was back with Mick and Terry when somebody noticed the smoke. The party got lively after that.

"Get the fire extinguishers," Allegro roared.

He damn well didn't want the fire department up there if he could help it. People were yelling and running around, some toward the kitchen and some toward the elevator.

I ran down the hallway and found Deena lying on a bed in her bra and panties. She was crying, and Raul was stroking her.

He turned and saw me and in one fluid motion was off the bed and facing me with a switchblade open in his hand.

"The place is on fire!" I yelled.

He smelled the smoke and was gone, hightailing it down the hall with his chartreuse shirttail flapping. I slapped Deena a few times and got her into her clothes.

By then they had the fire out, but there was still plenty of smoke. Allegro was yelling into the phone. Royce was up on the dais, nibbling the model's ear. A little smoke didn't bother him when romance beckoned. The preppy was out cold on the sofa. I left him there—the Colombians could screw him if they wanted to—and helped Deena to the elevator and down to the street.

I found a cab and dropped her at her parents' place on the West Side. She blubbered and thanked me and didn't make any sense. I hoped she'd forget the whole thing and forget Frazier Holloway, too. I was laughing inanely by the time I arrived at my hotel. It was one of Malloy's most famous victories, but he'd saved the wrong girl.

24

I was awakened by the phone the next morning. I felt like hell, but I grabbed it eagerly, wanting it to be Penny, but instead it was a fancy-sounding woman who said Mr. Draper wanted to see me. That was fine; I wanted to see him, too. I wanted to find out why he'd said Bonnie's call came from Times Square when—according to Elton—it had come from the Village. If he couldn't explain, I intended to go to Harry and find out if his "security consultant" was playing games.

"Can you come at once?" she pressed. "It's urgent. He's in room 723 at the Blanton Hotel, on 41st Street."

"I'm on my way," I promised.

I dressed in a hurry—no shave, no tie—and was fighting the mob in Times Square when I started to wonder how Draper, or his secretary, had known where to call me. But I'd given the number to Elton, and he'd given it to Linda, and probably Draper or Harry had gotten it from her.

The Blanton proved to be a dirty, depressing dump that no self-respecting junkie would OD in. Urgent, the woman had said; it must have been urgent to lure Lee Draper to a flophouse like this.

But wasn't this the sort of place where Bonnie might hide out?

I walked past the zombie at the desk to the elevator. A woman in a blood-red blouse stepped in ahead of me and punched seven, my floor. When she turned, I saw that she was forty or so, a junkie/hooker probably, a walking skeleton with bleached hair, bad skin plastered with cheap makeup, desperate eyes, and a "toilet water" that I thought would make me sick. The door closed, and I shuddered and punched six. I didn't want to get off on the same floor with her or look at her or smell her a moment longer than necessary.

In the sixth-floor hallway I leaned against the wall, staring numbly at the surreal wallpaper, huge undulating flowers poised to attack me. I was dizzy from too many days of too much booze and not enough food or sleep. When my heart stopped pounding, I took the stairs to seven.

I opened the door cautiously. I wasn't up to a face-to-face confrontation with the death-mask blonde. As I watched, she moved down the hallway, knocked on a door, then another, before someone admitted her. I didn't want to speculate on what her business might be. Instead, I stood motionless, peering through a crack in the door at room 723.

I should have crossed the hall, knocked on the door, and announced, "Draper, I'm here."

But I didn't.

Why? I don't know. Suspicion? A sixth sense? Good luck? Just say that everything about this squalid Heartbreak Hotel spooked me, from William Burroughs at the front desk to the skeleton in the elevator, and I was in no hurry to keep my appointment. So I watched the door for five minutes, in a kind of trance, and then the knob began to turn.

It turned very, very slowly, and the door opened even more slowly, and finally an eye appeared in the crack. Like someone thought the woman in red had been me and was wondering where the hell I'd gone.

It wasn't hard to figure out that the face I glimpsed wasn't Lee Draper's, because it was black.

I eased the door shut and tried to think. I might have hightailed it down the stairs, but I didn't trust my legs. Then I heard the siren.

The face in 723 heard it, too, because a moment later he came barreling out. He hit the stairs and blew past me as if I weren't there. I stepped into the hallway. The arrow over the elevator showed it was headed down, so I slipped into 723.

Lee Draper was stretched out on the bed, warm blood soaking his blue Brooksweave shirt. I shook him, making sure he was dead, and that was when I saw the cheap little revolver half-hidden under his body. It looked familiar, and I picked it up and realized it was damned familiar; it had last been seen under my mattress.

I ran to the window and saw the cop car in the street. Outside, the ancient elevator groaned and rattled like some medieval torture machine. I shoved the gun in my pocket and ran. I'd just shut the stairway door behind me when the elevator doors banged open. Through the crack I saw the ghostly desk clerk lead two of New York's finest to 723.

I raced down the stairs, past trash and vomit and comatose junkies, trying to make quick decisions. Out through the lobby or down a fire escape? Keep the gun or throw it away? There was no time for logic, so I opted for my old friend audacity. With the gun—my gun, the gun that had killed Lee Draper—in my pocket, I strolled through the deserted lobby, passed the empty police car, and hastened toward the blessed anonymity of Times Square.

I ducked into Nathan's, called my hotel again—still no message from Penny—and downed a bowl of chili and a beer. I thought hard—the prospect of a murder rap does tend to focus one's thoughts—and decided that (1) someone had found out where I was staying, (2) stolen my gun, (3) used it to kill Draper, and (4) tried to set me up.

If I'd barged into 723, I'd have been banged on

the head and left there, with a gun and a corpse, ready for the cops to haul away.

I wondered who had staged the setup, and then I wondered something even more interesting: Wouldn't it have been simpler just to kill me? Why go to all the trouble of a frame-up? It was like the beating I'd taken in the back of the cab. Somebody wanted me discouraged but didn't quite have the heart to kill me.

They were succeeding; I was discouraged as hell.

Before I left Nathan's, when I thought nobody was watching, I checked my revolver. I'd put six slugs in it before I left home. Sure enough, one was missing, the one that'd killed Draper. I slipped it into my belt. No more hiding it under my mattress. Mrs. Malloy's baby boy was going armed now.

Orth Butler kept an office in the Pan-Am Building. I called and caught him there.

"Grady, where are you? Harry and I have been looking everywhere."

"I'm not far away."

"Then come over here at once," Orth declared.

"Okay," I said. "I'll do that."

A gorgeous black secretary ushered me into the seventeenth-floor office, where Harry and Orth were waiting. Orth was in navy blue and Harry in gray pinstripes. They looked like what they were, two of the men who run America, who try to run the world. Orth hurried to take my arm.

"Good God, man, what's happened to you?" He eased me into a chair. I guessed I was a mess, unshaven, bewildered, with beer and chili on my breath.

"Lee Draper's dead," I said. "Somebody killed him and tried to blame me for it."

"The police just called about his death," Orth said. "Naturally I'm most concerned."

"Who did it?" Harry demanded. He had knelt beside me, staring into my eyes with a ferocity I'd never seen before.

"I don't know," I said. "A woman called—Draper's secretary, I guess—and said he wanted to meet me at a cheap hotel. He was there, dead. I barely got out before the police came. It was a setup."

I didn't tell them about the black man I'd glimpsed; it was instinct not to tell them everything I knew.

"What about the gun?" Harry asked.

"I threw it away." I was so pleased with my smooth lie that I neglected to ask the obvious question: What did he know about any gun?

"Lee didn't have a secretary," Orth said. "It certainly was an attempt to discredit you. Fortunately, it failed. You're sure no one saw you?"

I shrugged. The desk clerk had seen me. The bleached blonde had seen me. But what would they remember?

"Why would anyone want to kill Draper?" I asked.

"Lee had enemies," Harry said darkly. "He had his finger in a lot of pies."

A lot of pies indeed. I thought of Amanda and wondered if Draper's affair with her, if indeed there was one, led to his death, or was it quite irrelevant? There's an old Texas joke that says you don't mess with the sheriff's girl, but Draper probably never heard that one.

"Bonnie called Penny from New York the night Penny came up here," I said. "Draper told me he'd traced the call to a Times Square pay phone. But I have other information—a source I trust absolutely—that the call was placed from the Village. Why would he lie?"

"Where in the Village?" Orth demanded.

"I don't know," I admitted.

I was thinking it was odd they didn't press me about my source—they were not men who liked mysteries. Then, suddenly, I was thinking of the Village, starting to remember what I'd forgotten for so long. Something Bonnie had said weeks before, when we talked at Orso's, shot back into my consciousness, the way long-buried images from my childhood will shoot back, unsought, often unwelcome, as if my mind were some mad miswired computer—a good enough mind for a novelist but a lousy one for a detective.

"Lee could have gotten bad information from the phone company," Harry was saying. "Or your source could have."

I nodded vaguely, but my mind was elsewhere in the city, a certain block on a certain street, and I knew that was where I should be, not here. Why in God's name had it taken so long?

"What is it, Grady?" Orth asked. "What's wrong?"

"Nothing. I'm a little woozy, I guess."

Could I trust these people? Elton had said to trust no one. But Harry was an old friend, and Elton was CIA. Could I trust anyone?

"I'll call my doctor," Orth said.

"No, I've got to go," I protested.

"Nonsense, he can be here in five minutes. You don't look well."

They overcame my protests. The doctor gave me some pills and told me to go to bed for three days. I lay down on Orth's leather sofa and slept for an hour. A dream about screaming children awoke me, and they were still there.

"I've got to go," I said.

"You need rest," Harry said.

"No," I said, struggling to my feet. "I've—"

"Grady, there are some things that need explaining," Orth Butler said. He was seated behind his desk, a craggy, cold-eyed, square-jawed, powerful old man.

229

Orth was what God would have looked like if God was an old tycoon with an office in the Pan-Am Building.

I stood there in indecision, torn between what I had to do and what he wanted to tell me.

"I can explain about the missing cassette," Orth said, "and why this matter is of such urgent importance."

I sank into a chair.

"Have you ever heard of the Party of God?"

I thought of a couple of quips but stifled them and shook my head.

"It's an Iran-based Islamic extremist group, also known as Hezbollah," the old man said solemnly. "They're closely allied with the Islamic Jihad, the most extreme of the extremists. Their goal is the total extinction of Israel, and in recent months they have formulated a plan to that end."

"Is that what's on the tape?" I asked.

"Yes, it records a meeting of the Party of God's ruling council at which plans were discussed and promises made. Essentially, they contemplate a coordinated attack, a suicide attack, if you will, involving hundreds of thousands of fanatics. They don't care how many die. They don't care if they trigger a nuclear war. All they care about is sweeping Israel into the sea. That's what Harry and I are fighting to prevent."

I was thinking fast, trying to compare what he told me with what Uri had told me, trying to decide

230

if I believed him. Then I realized that I really didn't give a damn about the missing cassette. Whether or not Israel was swept into the sea was NMP, not my problem. My problem was finding my daughter, and now, finally, I knew where to look.

I stood up. "I've got to go," I said.

"Wait, we have more to tell you," Harry said.

"Later," I told him, and was gone.

25

From the corner of Bleecker and Thompson I could see half a dozen family-style restaurants, Chinese, Greek, Italian, French, Spanish.

It hit me while I was with Orth and Harry— Bonnie's story about her boyfriend, the nice guy who lived in the Village, the boy she'd lost because her beeper went off at the wrong time. She'd said his parents had a restaurant in the Village. She'd told me his name, too, and now it came back to me—Mario, like the governor. I call him Mike, she'd said.

Other pieces began to fit. Elton said Bonnie's call came from the Village. And Linda said that Penny had phoned from someplace noisy—a restaurant, perhaps.

So how many Italian restaurants were there in the Village? Plenty, but if Penny was hiding in one of them, I'd find her.

There was one across the street, Amari's. I could start there.

For a restaurant this was the midafternoon lull.

I looked in, saw no one, then stepped inside. I saw red-and-white tablecloths, a neat little bar, candles and fresh flowers, sparkling silverware, paintings of Italian fishing villages, but no people.

"Hello?" I called.

No answer.

At the side of the room was a counter with a cash register, cigarettes and candy, a door behind it, perhaps leading upstairs. I edged toward that door, again calling a nervous "Hello?"

When I opened the door, a scream filled my ears, and a blade flashed before my eyes.

I threw up one arm and fell back as the knife cut into my palm. I stumbled over a table, and still she was coming at me, wailing in Italian. I backed away, blood dripping from my hand. "Wait," I pleaded, "Wait."

She was between me and the front door, a small, stout woman; her graying hair was pulled back from a face that was red, tear stained, desperate. She came at me relentlessly, waving the knife before her, and if she didn't look experienced at homicide, she looked ready to learn.

I grabbed a napkin and wrapped it around my hand. She lunged again, backed me into a corner. I knew I could take her out with a chair if I had to, and that moment was not far distant.

"I'm a friend," I said. "I'm looking for Mario."

She muttered in Italian and jabbed at me with the

knife. I gave more ground. "I'm a friend of Bonnie's," I said. "Penny's father."

I reached for a chair. She still had the knife pointed at my heart, but her eyes met mine, and suddenly the fight went out of her. She sank into a chair, let the knife clatter to the floor, lowered her head to the tablecloth, and began to sob. I watched her warily, feeling the throb in my hand, seeing my blood soak the napkin, and sat down across from her.

"Where are they?" I asked.

The woman looked at me, her round face wet with tears. "You are Penny's father?"

"Yes."

"Come," she said.

She led me up the stairs, through a cluttered sitting room with a TV, lace curtains, overstuffed chairs, trophies, religious ornaments, and family pictures, and into a shadowy bedroom.

The man on the bed was wiry and white haired, but more than that I could not tell. His face was a battered, bloody mess. One eye was closed, and his nose looked like putty. A portly man with a beard was ministering to him. He said something in Italian and began to set the nose.

"What happened?" I asked.

"A man came and beat him," the woman told me.

"Have you called an ambulance?"

"This is Dr. Gregario; he will treat him."

"What about the police?"

The woman's eyes flashed angrily. "No police."

We heard footsteps; then Bonnie burst into the room with a dark, muscular youth. The boy saw the man on the bed and let out a cry. He knelt and took the man's hand and whispered to him. The man muttered back between his broken teeth.

Bonnie threw her arms around me. She was wearing jeans, a baggy sweatshirt, no makeup; she'd never looked better. I hugged her tight, and she began to cry.

The doctor spoke to us, adjusted the lamp, and reached into his bag. He was going to start the stitches, and he wanted us out. We retreated to the sitting room, Bonnie and I, with the youth I took to be Mario, and the woman I took to be his mother.

"This is Mr. Malloy," Bonnie said.

"Who did this to my father?" the boy demanded.

"A very large, dark man with a beard," the woman said. "He came with two other men and asked where you and the girls were. Your father told them to go away. They beat him, seeking information, but he would tell them nothing. I believe they would have killed him, but Penny returned."

"Penny—what happened, where is she?" I cried.

"The men took her away," the woman said. "She fought them, but they threw a blanket over her and carried her out."

I reeled from the news. Nick Allegro, seeking the

tape, had beaten the old man, then carried off my daughter.

"Bonnie, for God's sake, why didn't you and Penny call me?" I demanded.

"We did. We called and called. But they kept saying you weren't checked in."

"Who said that?" I yelled.

"The Algonquin. We called—"

"Dammit, I wasn't staying at the Algonquin!" I raged. I'd told Elton where I was. How the hell could he have gotten it screwed up?

The boy's face burned like a flame. He looked at Bonnie, then at me. "Who is he?" he demanded. "Where is he?"

Bonnie gasped. She knew who the attacker had been, just as I did. But she shook her head. "I don't know, Mario," she said. "I honest to God don't know."

I understood. She didn't want her lover going up against Allegro and his boys. Who could blame her?

The boy seized my arm. "Who was he?"

"I don't know," I said. "But I've got to go. I've got to find Penny."

"I'll come with you," Mario said.

"No," I said. "Stay with your mother and father."

"We have friends," the boy said. "We will find them and kill them."

I didn't doubt his sincerity—I had a feeling his

236

friends were Sicilian—but I didn't have time to wait for them to get organized. "What about the tape?" I said. "Where is it?"

Bonnie gasped. "Penny had it."

"With her? In her purse?"

"I think so."

I ran down the stairs and left them there. I wished I could have taken Mario with me. He looked like a tough kid. But his mother had been through enough for one day. What I had to do I would have to do alone.

26

I sweated blood on the long ride uptown. I looked out at the people and the traffic and the buildings, and it was all surreal; so many faces, so many dramas, so many comedies and tragedies, more than the mind could comprehend, and who gave a damn if this girl was raped or that man beaten or murdered? Life flowed on in all its savage, glorious indifference.

An afternoon tabloid lying on the seat provided a moment's diversion: Lee Draper's death was headlined on page 3, with a picture. Noted political consultant, Yale grad, ex-Senate aide, murdered in Times Square hotel, hint of scandal. A sorry ending for a stylish fellow.

Not my problem except that my gun had killed him and I was still toting it around.

Horns honked, gridlock grabbed, questions maddened. How had Nick Allegro found Bonnie's hideout only minutes before I did? Why was someone always a step ahead of me? If Allegro had gotten the tape from Penny, why had he taken her with him?

That thought chilled me. I knew how young women fared at Allegro's stronghold. I had no time for police or search warrants or proof. I thought of stopping to call Uri, but in my frenzy I didn't want even to waste the minutes that would take. Faster, I told the driver, faster! I tossed him a couple of twenties, and he started running red lights. I clutched the gun beneath my coat, hoping it would solve some problems, too.

The day had grown windy; rain was coming. When we finally arrived uptown, I confronted the fortress of Allegro's apartment building, and the first drops began to fall. I saw the guard in the lobby. Even if I overpowered him, there'd be another armed goon waiting when the elevator stopped at Allegro's floor. I thought of tales to tell, to lie my way past the guards, but they all seemed destined to fail. As I watched from across the street, undecided, three dark-haired youths in bright shirts piled out of a cab and jitterbugged into the lobby. I had to act, even if it meant trying to shoot my way in, and then I saw the paint truck.

It was parked beside the building, an old blue panel truck with "Bigham and Son" on its side. Two men in overalls were loading ladders and dropcloths into it, father and son by the looks of them. I walked up to them.

"Excuse me," I said. "Are you Mr. Bigham?"

The older man studied me uneasily. I still had the bloody napkin knotted around my left palm. "That's right."

"Did you just paint Mr. Allegro's kitchen?" I asked.

"That's right. He had hisself a fire."

"He's a friend of mine," I said. "I have a big job I need done. Let me take a look at what you did for him. If it looks good, you can paint my apartment."

"If he's your friend, mister, why don't you go up the front way?" the younger man demanded.

"I don't want to bother him," I said.

"We done finished for today. We's just locking up," the father said.

I pulled some bills from my pocket. "Here's a five-hundred-dollar deposit," I said. "I'd like a quick look at his kitchen. Just loan me the key. I'll lock the door when I leave."

Nobody was fooling anybody now. The older man looked longingly at the money, then said, "Can't do it. We bonded. Can't get involved in nothing like that."

"Daddy, it's easy money," his son said.

"Don't matter."

"Five hundred, cash. Right now. You just give me the key and go about your business."

"Easy money," the son repeated. I liked his attitude.

"Dammit, boy, we got a business. You know who

lives up there. We don't want no part of that fellow."

I was about to pull my gun when I had another idea. I took an old White House pass from my billfold. "I'm a federal agent," I said. "I need that key."

The old man gulped. "Yes, sir," he said, and handed me his ring of keys.

"Wait up," the son said. "What about the money?"

I gave him the wad of bills. "Just start driving and don't look back."

The son pocketed the money and pulled his father toward the truck.

Could I trust them? Would they alert Allegro? I thought that anybody halfway smart would take the money and run, and they looked smart enough. As soon as their truck rattled away, I entered a door marked No Trespassing and took the elevator up.

The ride was slow, the elevator smelly. It stopped, finally, on the eighteenth floor, Allegro's floor. I stepped into a small, dark hallway half-filled with trash bags and empty bottles, listened at the door, and inserted the key.

The freshly painted kitchen was empty, but the dishwasher was humming. I heard sounds ahead, music, laughter, cries, groans, the clank of metal, the rumble of thunder outside. Penny was here somewhere, of that I was sure, Despite a gnawing fear, I eased along the hallway until I reached a half-open door. Three men were working out on Nautilus machines; they didn't notice as I slipped past. The jukebox was playing the Doors' "Light My Fire," a favorite of Penny's. Where the hell was she?

I heard a woman crying. I pushed open one of the bedroom doors and found a dark-skinned woman sobbing into a pillow. It was the Eurasian beauty I'd seen at Ruth's. She looked at me, through me, lost in her private sorrow. Her smooth nut-colored body was covered with ugly red welts. I shut the door and moved toward the music.

The record changed. The Stones' "You Can't Always Get What You Want," another of her favorites. I kept going until I reached the big room where Allegro held court. Dusk had come; the room was smoky and dim, and rain pelted the windows. To my right, four Latins were playing cards near the jukebox. One of them was Raul, the smoothie with the mustache, still wearing his chartreuse shirt. A couple of pouting girls sat nearby, watching a game show on a portable TV. They couldn't hear it for the jukebox; they just watched the wheel spinning and the prizes and bright colors and the winners jumping up and down.

To my left, thirty feet away, Nick Allegro was sitting on his dais in a peach-colored chair. Across from him, on a white sofa, sat Penny. I was taken aback; she was smiling, talking animatedly, looking relaxed and lovely, her blonde hair swirling about her sky-blue sweater. She was smoking a cigarette and sipping a glass of wine, and Allegro held a beer.

I studied the logistics. I had to assume all the men were armed. Once I entered the room, I would be caught in a crossfire between them. I had five shots in my revolver; I needed a machine gun.

There was no time to hesitate; the weight lifters were behind me, and others might come. Although I'd been a mere nonviolent clerk during my army years, I knew one military axiom: Take the high ground. I was nonviolent no more. Not now. I took a deep breath and walked in as though I owned the place.

Penny saw me first, her lips parting in disbelief. Then I was on the dais, my gun leveled at Allegro.

"Move and I'll blow your head off."

Penny jumped up and grabbed my arm. "Daddy, it's okay, really. Nobody's hurt me. We're just waiting for—"

The card players leaped to their feet. "Down!" I yelled, waving my gun at them. Raul reached into his pocket, and I fired, a lucky shot, and he dropped to his knees, clutching his gut. His friends hit the deck.

Four shots left. Allegro glared at me but didn't move. I thought my best hope of getting out of there was to use him for a hostage. That meant taking him down the elevator with us, which was like climbing in a closet with a bear, but it was the best I could do.

243

"Up," I said. Allegro's eyes burned with perfect hate as he rose to his feet.

I watched him with a certain satisfaction, and then I saw a blur across the room. I turned and saw another of the card players aiming at me. I fired wildly, Mick Jagger abruptly shut up, and Allegro charged like a bull.

Penny saved me. She threw herself at his ankles, like an open-field tackler, and he crashed at my feet.

I waved my gun at the card players, and at the same time I took a couple of steps and place kicked Allegro's head, just below the ear. He howled with pain, the sweetest music I'd ever heard.

"Get down, Penny," I cried. We knelt, half-hidden behind Allegro's bulk, as his goons fanned out across the room. I grabbed his hair with one hand and jabbed the working end of my revolver into his ear.

"One little bullet, one little brain," I said. "Get up real slow."

I saw the Latins moving again. "Get back down or I'll kill him," I yelled. I only had a few seconds before I was going to have to shoot someone.

Then a booming voice filled the room:

"GRADY, ALL OF YOU, STOP THIS AT ONCE!"

Everyone froze; then Orth Butler came striding

toward me as calmly as he would enter the Plaza for lunch.

"You men, put your guns away," he told the Latins. "Leave the room. It's all right now."

The Colombians backed out the door, dragging the groaning, gut-shot Raul with them. Lightning crashed nearby as the storm broke over the city.

Orth ascended the dais. I still had my revolver in Allegro's bloody ear.

"Get up, Grady, it's all right now."

"What are you doing here?" I didn't move the gun.

"Grady, your daughter is safe, we've recovered the tape, we've found Bonnie—everything is fine. We can go now." He had changed into tweeds since I'd seen him last. "Put the gun away."

I didn't put it away. "Baby, are you all right?"

"Yes, Daddy, really. We just, you know, talked and played records. They knew you'd come."

I didn't understand what she meant. I didn't understand anything. Allegro heaved to his feet like a wounded elephant. "Get this bastard out of here or I'll kill him," he bellowed.

"I'll do the killing, asshole," I muttered.

"Stop it, both of you," Orth said. "Nick, you should be ashamed of yourself if a middle-aged writer can bust in here and take over."

"Get him out of here," Allegro repeated. I

wondered if he might charge again and if three shots from a Saturday night special would bring him down. I was game to find out.

"Let's go, Grady," Orth said.

"Go where?" I asked. I had my arm around Penny, my eyes on Allegro, my gun pointed at his heart.

"Harry and I want to finish our discussion," he said. "We owe you an explanation."

27

There were more of Allegro's thugs in the lobby, but they parted like the Red Sea as Orth marched past, leading us out into the storm. His limo waited at the curb, and we gladly scrambled into the backseat. Soon enough I would regret that move, but right then Orth's limo looked like our salvation. His driver was a trim, dapper black man in a pearl-gray uniform; he'd driven me somewhere years before, and we'd talked about Coleman Hawkins.

The car slid into the night, and Orth said, "I think we'd all breathe more easily if you'd put that gun away. In the glove compartment, perhaps."

I laughed grimly. I had stuck the gun in my belt, but my hand was still on it.

"Recent events have made me a gun nut, Orth. You'll have to pry my cold, dead fingers off this weapon. It's one man's answer to the arms race."

He grumbled but didn't argue. The rain beat down. Suddenly, the Triborough Bridge loomed ahead. I'd thought the Waldorf was our destination. "Where are we going?"

"Up to Sleepy Harbor," Orth said. "Harry is waiting for us there."

Sleepy Harbor was Orth's estate on the Long Island Sound, up above Mamaroneck. I'd been there once for a fat-cat reception celebrating Harry's election to the Senate. It was a spectacular place, a bootlegger's dream house, straight out of the Roaring Twenties.

"I've been there," Penny said. "The summer Bonnie and I were nine. We rode and swam and explored; it was like a castle in a fairy tale. Do you live there now, Mr. Butler?"

The old man smiled. "No, my dear. I haven't lived there for years. We lease it out to, oh, private foundations, charitable groups, for retreats. But with things the way they are, it's a useful hideaway."

"I . . . what do you mean, Orth?" I asked.

"The Arabs, of course. I don't know what they're up to. They're devious people. But we'll be secure at Sleepy Harbor."

Penny was between me and Orth. A couple of times she gave me a look, as if there were something she wanted to tell me, but all I could do was nod and wait.

"What are you doing mixed up with Allegro?" I asked Butler. "He's a drug dealer and a killer."

"He's useful," Butler said. "You become spoiled

in government with various agencies at your disposal. On the outside you take what you can get."

"You can't trust him," I said.

"I don't trust him. But I know his superiors, and he respects their wishes."

I didn't ask who Allegro's superiors were; I was afraid I knew.

"You have the tape?"

"Yes, your daughter took excellent care of it." He patted Penny's hand. "You're a very clever young woman, my dear, very clever."

I could have told him that. "Where's Bonnie now?" Penny asked abruptly.

"I've had someone drive her and her young man down to Washington," Orth said smoothly.

That sounded odd. Mario didn't seem like someone Orth would encourage, nor would I have thought the boy would have left New York until he'd settled with whoever clobbered his father. I wanted to ask questions, a lot of questions, but Orth was gazing grimly out into the storm, tired of my carping, no doubt. I took Penny's hand and held it tight. In twenty minutes or so we slowed down, and a flash of lightning revealed the two well-armed men who were swinging open the big iron gates to Sleepy Harbor. It was then that I wondered if I'd escaped from the frying pan into the fire.

The estate sprawled over several hundred wooded acres. A long gravel driveway led to the big, terraced main house, and on the other side the lawn sloped down a half mile to a beach and boat docks on the Sound. We stopped in front of the Italianate mansion, and Orth led us up tile steps lined by life-size statues of Roman gods and goddesses.

When we reached the portico, out of the downpour, I said, "We'd like to get back to the city tonight, Orth. Will this take long?"

"Nonsense. You can stay here, and my pilot will fly you to Washington in the morning, after this storm passes."

Harry opened the door, in slacks and a Fair Isle sweater, grinning, pumping my hand. "It's all right," he kept saying. "Hey, it's all right."

He hugged Penny, told her how brave she was, what a great job she'd done. She said she wanted to go to bed, and Orth summoned a butler to take her upstairs. Then he led me and Harry into his library. It was a big, shadowy, pretentious room, all mahogany and leather and gold, that housed a lifetime's mementos: a lion's head over the mantle, elephant tusks, jade Buddahs, Oriental screens, and Impressionist paintings he'd bought for a song after the war.

"We'll have a drink," he said. "Then they can bring us chowder and sandwiches, if that's agreeable."

I stripped off my wet coat and warmed myself at the fire. "I need to call home," I told my host, whose butler was helping him into a burgundy smoking jacket.

Orth scowled. "Grady, as I've indicated, I'm concerned about security. Until this matter is fully resolved, I don't think we should call out or otherwise advertise our whereabouts."

Glaring back into his hard, impassive face, I faced a quick decision: Challenge him or play along?

I ended the tension by saying, "Sure, no problem."

Harry loudly announced that we should all have a drink.

When we were settled before the fire, sipping twelve-year-old scotch, Orth said, "This has been a most perplexing matter, Grady. Most perplexing."

I waited.

"Harry and I told you a bit about the missing cassette the other night, you'll recall. But as you might imagine, there's a good deal more to the story."

"I thought there might be," I said, trying to restrain my natural sarcasm. *Play dumb*, a little voice kept telling me. *You never get hurt playing dumb.*

"The Party of God does exist and does dream of destroying Israel, but the matter at hand is rather more complex. What I'm about to tell you may sound unbelievable, but take my word that it is true."

I shivered, as if with a premonition of what was to come.

"To put it bluntly," he continued, "the issue at hand is not the survival of Israel but the survival of America."

251

He paused to let that sink in. I tried to look awed. Harry's eyes were darting between us like a spectator at a tennis match.

"Israel could possibly be defeated by a coordinated pan-Arab attack," Orth continued. "But America will without question be defeated, within the next thirty years, not by nuclear attack or an enemy invasion but simply by economic rot. By the balance-of-trade deficit, the national debt, the collapse of the stock market, lost jobs, renewed inflation, an ever diminishing standard of living, and of course the greed of gutless politicians. These things will lead to economic decline and political chaos. At best we will become a second-class power, and at worst we will be conquered by stronger, more vital nations."

There was much truth to what he said. Any fool could see that the other nations were claiming more of the world's wealth and we were destined to have less, but it had never seemed to me (campaign rhetoric aside) that there was much to be done about it.

Harry broke in. "There's only one hope for us," he said. "Only one way to reverse the tide. I imagine you know what I mean."

"I'm not sure," I said truthfully. I wasn't sure just how crazy they were. I know people who think legal marijuana is America's only hope for survival.

"Oil!" Harry said.

Yes, of course, what else? A wave of relief swept through me, for suddenly all this made sense.

"We're running out of oil," Orth said. "The Arabs have it, and they'll bleed us dry, even as the Japanese steal hundreds of thousands of jobs, entire industries, away from us."

"But what can we do?" I asked.

I'd given him his cue, and after a dramatic pause the old man threw down the gauntlet: "We can internationalize the oil fields."

"Internationalize them?" I repeated. I liked the word; it had a certain grandeur to it. In my radical youth I had argued that our government should nationalize the American oil industry, but Orth's was clearly a grander concept, one that had not occurred to me and my fuzzy-minded friends.

"Oil is a resource that belongs to all the people of the world," Orth said. "Just like air, or sunshine."

I dared not smile. On the one hand, the scene had become hilarious as this old robber baron mouthed New Left clichés. But on the other hand (as editorial writers love to say), the game was deadly serious. These people were telling me things I didn't want to know, and I had no idea why.

"Ours is an oil-consuming nation," Orth continued. "If we require two-thirds of the world's oil, then as a matter of right and justice we should have two-thirds, at cost."

"You see, Grady," Harry interrupted, "it's only an accident of geography that the major oil reserves are located in the Arab world. The Arabs have no right to put their greed above the legitimate needs of the industrialized nations. The twenty-first century must place justice above geography."

"Justice above geography"—there was a line from an inaugural address if I ever heard one. And "an accident of geography," that was swell, too.

They were explaining their crackpot notions slowly, simply, as if to a child, and like a good child, I tried to look grateful. The realities of the matter were ever more clear: I had fallen in with madmen, and they had all the guns.

Well, not *all* the guns, since I still had three shots left in my six-shooter. Or was it two?

The butler brought in steaming bowls of clam chowder, a heaping platter of club sandwiches, and cold bottles of Bass ale. I asked about Penny, and he said she was asleep.

Orth attacked his sandwich ferociously, while Harry picked at his. I was trying to puzzle out the chemistry between them. As always, when they were together, Orth was the dominant figure, Harry the junior partner. That, I thought, was because, deep in his heart, Harry shared the old tycoon's view that to possess two hundred million dollars was a hell of a lot more important than to be a U.S. senator.

But something else, something more subtle, was in the air. I felt I was being given a test—one I in no way understood—and Harry was hoping I'd pass and Orth didn't give a damn.

We ate in silence. When Orth was finished, he called the butler to clear the plates and bring us coffee and brandy; then he resumed his lecture.

"Do you begin to see the equation, Grady?" he asked. "I want to save my country, to secure its future. I'm an old man and a rich man. I won't suffer. But I care about your daughters' generation, and generations yet unborn."

"How do we go about achieving internationalization?" I asked meekly.

He smiled like an old wolf. "The obvious thing would be simply to invade—just send our boys in and occupy the oil fields, but of course it's not that easy; nothing ever is. There would be two problems. First, the Russians could hardly be expected to sit by idly while we seized the world's oil supply. Second, and less important, would be the problem of American and world opinion."

"It would be tricky," Harry injected. "Imagine that America woke up one morning to the news that our troops were occupying the Arab oil fields and that one result would be the return of gasoline to fifty cents a gallon. You'd have protests, but you'd have support, too."

"You'd have plenty of support," I said. "If the American people would accept a ten-year war in Vietnam, with fifty thousand lives lost and nothing to win but rice paddies, they'd dance in the streets at the prospect of capturing the world's oil supply."

I wasn't kidding. Two decades in Washington had convinced me that with enough money, audacity, and TV time you could sell the American people anything.

"It would have to be properly presented," Harry said. He smiled and added, "Of course, that's your specialty."

"It's perfectly clear," I declared with a burst of enthusiasm. "To internationalize the Middle East oil fields we need three things. The military might, which obviously we have. Second, an understanding with the Russians, which I gather you think is not impossible. Third, an explanation, a rationale, to explain the move at home and abroad."

"Exactly," Harry said. "I knew you'd understand."

"All of which brings us back to the tape we've only just recovered," Orth said impatiently. "The tape was of a telephone conversation—a most indiscreet conversation—between Harry and Lee Draper in which Harry discussed Operation Sunrise, as we've termed this enterprise. We learned that Draper had recorded the conversation and was dealing secretly with the Saudis. He was able to deliver the tape to Khalid Yassin soon after his arrival in New York. My agents sought to retrieve the tape that same night and would have but for a most unfortunate and unlikely coincidence."

"You mean the fact that Bonnie was in Monica's apartment, and escaped with the tape," I said.

"Precisely," Orth said coldly.

"But now you have the tape back and everything's okay." I thought a minute. "Unless anyone made a copy of it."

"We spoke at length with Mr. Draper before his death," Orth said, "and we are persuaded that he did not make a copy. And I'm quite sure that Yassin did not, or his colleagues in Saudi intelligence would have behaved quite differently since his passing."

"Then you're home free," I said. "Because only Bonnie and Penny have had it since then."

Once I spoke the words, I saw them hanging frozen in the air before my face, then crash to the floor and shatter like glass. Bonnie and Penny. Girls at play.

"Let's assume our daughters played the tape while they had it," Harry said. He stood before the big fireplace, outlined in flame. "Maybe the boy Mario, too. They're young, impressionable kids, with no understanding of the world. What they heard might have confused them, upset them. So it's our job to calm them down. They've blundered into information that could be harmful to them, don't you see?"

"Yes, of course," I whispered. I saw all too clearly. You could erase a tape, but how did you erase three minds?

"We talked to Bonnie this afternoon, and she

assures me they made no copy," Harry added. "Of course, you might want to double-check that with Penny."

I nodded weakly.

Orth heaved himself to his feet. "Let's be rid of the damn thing," he declared. He pulled the cassette from his pocket and yanked the tape until yards of it dangled from his hands. Then, with an angry gesture, he tossed the whole mess into the flames. We watched in silence as the tape melted and was gone.

Orth turned back and glared at me. "I'm about to explain Operation Sunrise to you," he said gruffly. "Fewer than ten men in the world know what you are about to hear."

It was an honor I devoutly wished I could decline. But I couldn't. Penny and I were in this together now.

"In a year, Harry will be the president-elect," Orth said. "I have no doubt of it. He is a credible candidate, and we have the money to elect him.

"Once Harry is president, Operation Sunrise will follow quickly. Hezbollah, the Party of God, will be given a low-yield nuclear device, which it will set off in Tel Aviv. That detonation will be immediately followed by a massive land assault on Israel. The Israelis will respond with nuclear weapons of their own, but those weapons, while they may devastate certain Arab capitals, will do little to stop a suicide attack coming from every direction. Suddenly the world will face a regional nuclear war—one that apparently could engulf the entire world—as well as hundreds of thousands dead and the prospect of the house-to-house slaughter of every man, woman, and child in Israel."

"My God," I muttered.

"At that point," Orth continued, "the American president and the Soviet premier will launch a joint U.S.-Soviet military action to halt the Hezbollah invasion. We will use whatever force is required to turn back the invaders. We and the Soviets will proceed to occupy the Arab states and oversee the internationalization of their oil resources. At that point, we will be seen not as invaders but rather as saviors of world peace."

"The Israeli government will agree to this?" I asked.

"It is not necessary that the entire government know of or agree to the plan," Orth said. "Only that certain key elements assent to it. Those elements, needless to say, will be in power when our operation is complete."

"But they'll lose thousands of people," I protested.

Harry smiled serenely. "Israel will lose some people, yes. But they're losing people already, year after year, being bled to death. How many more decades can they hang on, the way things are? I tell you, the realists in Israel, the men who take the long view, thank God for Operation Sunrise."

"Dammit, man, look what we'll have accomplished when the dust settles!" Orth declared. "The Arab nations will be prostrate, no longer a military threat to Israel, to one another, or to world peace. International terrorism will have been eliminated in one fell swoop. Oil supplies to the industrial nations will be guaranteed, at a fair price, for decades to come. And, finally, the U.S. and Russia will have entered a new era, partners, saviors of the entire world. I predict that the success of Operation Sunrise will lead, before Harry completes his first term, to major arms reductions, which in turn will lead to peace and prosperity for all the world."

"A century of peace," Harry declared.

"A century of peace," I echoed numbly.

Harry knelt beside me. "Grady, *it must be done.* There is a price in lives, yes, but the alternative is the destruction of Israel and the eventual collapse of the United States. I, as president, can't let that happen."

Harry had bought it. The light of true belief burned in his eyes. A lot could happen, but it looked at least fifty-fifty that Harry would be elected president, Orth would be pulling his strings, and Operation Sunrise would proceed on schedule.

"Look at the big picture," Harry said, warming to the subject. "Israel is surrounded by hostile Arab states; any fool can see that. But we, the U.S., are also surrounded by a hostile world. They face military defeat; we face economic defeat. Our fates are absolutely joined. And the Russians face the same economic threats we do—we're natural allies, once we break the shackles of ideology."

Yes, that ideology is a bitch, I thought. *It keeps telling you that Jefferson makes more sense than Lenin and that invading other countries isn't the American way.* But what I said was "You're right. It's hard, but it's necessary. It's historic . . . It's like the Marshall Plan."

"Exactly," Harry said. He beamed at my words of approval. But Orth's canny old face was carved from ice.

"Could I ask one question?" I said.

"Of course," Harry replied.

"Given the Israeli military might, could any sort of Arab ground attack, suicide attack, whatever its size, have a chance of success?"

Harry smiled. "You see, Grady, for our purposes, the question is not whether the attack could succeed but whether the various Arab extremist groups *believe* it could, whether they're willing to launch it."

"In other words, whether they're crazy enough to try?"

Harry looked pained. "Perhaps it's not so crazy if you believe that to die in holy war is to awake in paradise. It's their religion, Grady."

"Yes, of course."

"Don't worry about the details," he said. "You've got your work cut out for you. I've got to get elected, and I want you with me, all the way.

Speech writer, director of communications, hell, you can write my memoirs when the time comes. Boy, what a time we'll have."

"It sounds wonderful," I said. "An honor." I raised my glass of brandy. "To Operation Sunrise." Harry and I clinked glasses, but Orth only heaved himself to his feet.

"It's late," he said. "We'll be up early in the morning to fly Grady and his daughter home. I'll show you to your room, Grady."

"Don't bother," I protested.

"It's no bother. Harry, you wait here. There's one final matter we need to discuss."

We stepped into the hall. I saw the man on duty at the front door and another peering out of the kitchen. As we climbed the stairs to my third-floor room, I heard the howl of the wind outside, the angry rumble of thunder. I'd forgotten the storm while we were in the library.

We reached my room, and he pushed open the door. "I trust you'll be comfortable here," he said. "Your daughter is just down the hall, in Bonnie's old room."

I put my hand on his arm. "Orth, I truly appreciate your confidence in me. I'll . . . I'll try to live up to it. What you're doing is terribly important."

"Yes," he said. "Sleep well."

28

His footsteps receded down the stairs. Thunder rolled and broke outside, punctuated by the sound of a shutter banging as relentlessly as a hammer. When Orth was gone, I tried the door and found it unlocked. Lights burned on the landing, and muffled voices rose up from below. I could leave my room, but I didn't think it would be so easy to leave the house.

I wanted to find Penny, but I needed to think first. I went to the window. Rain danced against the glass, and the shutter swung crazily. Lightning broke above the lawn, the statues, the dark forest, and I wondered how many armed men were down there, waiting in the storm.

The doorknob turned. As I fumbled for my gun, Penny burst in. She ran to my arms, young and strong, bursting with life.

"Oh, Daddy, I got you into this," she whispered.

"No, I got myself into it."

"When you had me," she said, forcing a smile,

brushing her dirty-blonde hair back from her tear-bright face.

"Daddy, we listened to the tape. Mr. Prescott and Mr. Butler have this crazy plan to blow up half the world."

"They told me."

"Can they really do that?" she asked. "Start a war and take over the oil fields?"

"It's possible," I told her. "If you have nuclear weapons, almost anything is possible. But that's not our problem."

Her sweet face darkened. "What do you mean?"

To tell her the truth or try to spare her? It wasn't a hard decision. We were in this together. Besides, she might have some ideas, and I was running short.

"I tried to sound like I'd go along with them. Be the PR man for their goddamn World War Three. That's what Harry wants."

She kissed my hand. "Poor Daddy."

"I figure they're down there now, debating what to do about me. About us. Harry's the sentimental type, he wants to trust me, but Orth knows better. He'll say I can't be trusted, and he'll win the debate."

Yeah, I thought, *high-minded Harry will reluctantly let himself be persuaded; then the son of a bitch will sleep better because he gave me a chance.*

"But what will they do?"

I looked her in the eye. "It comes down to this.

We know about their plot. Either they trust us, or they kill us."

"My God, Daddy," she cried as my words sank in. Then she added, as if it might somehow help, "Bonnie knows, too."

"Bonnie is a different matter. She's Harry's daughter, easier for him to persuade—and harder for him to kill. With all her problems, they'd probably just put her away for a while."

"What are we going to do?"

"We can do nothing and hope I'm wrong. But I've got to be honest with you. I don't think they plan for us to make it home in the morning."

"What would they do?"

I shrugged. "A car wreck? A plane crash? Some kind of accident, probably."

"I went downstairs while you were still in the library. There were four men in the kitchen, drinking coffee. They'd been out in the rain and were taking a break. They all had these . . . these *machine guns.*"

"That's great," I said. "And I've got my trusty six-shooter." I showed it to her.

"Is that the one you kept in the old sneaker in the back of your closet?"

"How'd you know?"

"Oh, Daddy, you used to hide your dope there, too. So symbolic—dope in one sneaker and a gun in the other, like the sword and the olive branch."

There's no privacy for a father. "Okay, let's think this through. I've got three shots left. Not much fire-power up against that army down there."

"Maybe you could take Mr. Butler hostage," she suggested. "Like you did Nick Allegro."

"I don't think they'd let me pull that twice. What they'll do is be all sweetness and light, give us break-fast, get us out of the house, and then zap us on the way to the airport. So, if I'm right, we have tonight to get out of here. Except I don't know how."

The knock at the door made me jump. I motioned Penny into the bathroom. "Who is it?"

"Me," Harry said.

"Come on in."

Harry entered with a weary smile. "The room okay?"

"Yeah, great."

We faced each other awkwardly. Had Orth told him I was armed? Or did they think I was so dumb it didn't matter? "Grady, I just want to say . . . Well, I know our plan sounds *extreme* the first time you hear it, but it's the only answer. America can't curl up and die for lack of oil."

"Harry, I told you, I agree with you."

He seemed unpersuaded. "Well, I just want to say, however things work out, that I've always thought a hell of a lot of you. You and Linda and Penny, too. You're wonderful people. The best."

266

"You, too," I said. "You'll make a great president."

He shrugged uneasily. "Well, thanks for everything. To Penny, too. Is she—?"

"She's asleep. You can tell her in the morning."

"Yeah, sure." He summoned his most telegenic grin. "Well, good night, Grady. God bless you."

He extended his hand. For one sweet moment I thought about shooting him, right then and there. It would have made me feel a hell of a lot better, but the trouble was it wouldn't have done me any good. Orth's goons would have come running and had a good excuse to gun me down. I had to be more devious than that. So instead of shooting him, I shook his hand.

He truly looked unhappy, far more than I, which was pretty funny if you thought about it. The thing was, I still thought I had a chance, and Harry knew he didn't. He'd sold his soul. Harry's curse was that he was intelligent enough to know he was wrong, decent enough to care, but not strong enough to resist.

After he left, Penny said, "What was that all about?"

"I think my old friend was telling me that he sincerely regrets our forthcoming demise."

She inexplicably grinned. "Daddy, I just remembered, I know a way out of here."

"You what?"

"Come on."

She led me to the door. We heard voices, and we stood there a long time, not sure if it was safe to go out. Finally, when all was quiet downstairs, when we could see only shadows, hear only the rattle and wail of the storm, she took my hand and guided me through the darkness to her room.

It was a Victorian bedroom with a four-poster, ruffled curtains, and a single antique lamp burning beside the bed. The walls were a pale pink and covered with horse pictures.

Penny gently shut the door behind us. "We had this whole floor when I was here before," she whispered. "We used to spend all our time exploring—this place is like a haunted house. You know what we found?"

"What?"

She opened a closet door and motioned me over. "Do you remember a book called *The Lion, the Witch and the Wardrobe*? There was a closet that opened into another world. It's like that here; we found a secret staircase. The man who built the house, the bootlegger? I think this was his escape hatch. Come on."

She lit a candle and handed it to me. Then, before my disbelieving eyes, she slid back a panel in the rear of the closet. "Open sesame," she murmured.

We bent low and passed through the opening; then she closed the panel behind us. In the dim, dancing candlelight I saw we were at the top of a narrow staircase. "Where does this go?"

"Down to the basement. Then there's a tunnel out to a cottage. Bonnie used it for a playroom."

The first step creaked; it was like a fire alarm going off. "Daddy, for God's sake!"

We went down, down, down in the darkness, slowly, uncertainly. The narrow steps twisted back and forth. It was a fun house, an endless journey, and then we saw a sliver of light ahead.

I crept up to it and peered through a narrow vertical crack. Penny was beside me, trying to push me out of the way. "What is it?" she demanded.

"Hush!"

I was looking into a pantry, past a shelf of pots and canned goods, into a big kitchen where Orth and Harry were sitting side by side at a table, drinking coffee and talking in low, conspiratorial tones. Again the urge to homicide welled up inside me, and again I fought it down.

Penny pushed me aside to take a look. She cursed at the two men, and I tugged at her to come on. While they were plotting our deaths, we could make our escape.

"Let's go," I told her.

"No, look!"

I put my eye to the crack again. A new figure had come into view. Orth Butler was standing, talking to Nick Allegro. I couldn't hear them, but the look on

Allegro's face told me what he was saying: He wanted me. That was fine; I wanted him, too.

Our stub of candle showed the stairway taking another twist downward. I turned to go, but Penny wanted a last look into the kitchen. I can't explain what happened next. Maybe she bumped me, maybe I lost my balance, but one of us banged into the wall and there was a tremendous racket as dozens of pots and pans crashed to the pantry floor.

"Oh, hell!" Penny cried.

"Let's go," I said.

We clattered down the stairs. I didn't know if they'd find the panel right away, but they'd sure as hell check our rooms and be after us soon.

Abruptly the stairs ended, and we had a brief glimpse of a low stone-walled tunnel that shot into the distance. Then our candle died, and the tunnel was as dark as a tomb.

Penny lit a match, and we stumbled ahead. Soon we gave up on matches and raced along in the darkness with our hands in front of us. We collided with a wall, lit another match, and found a ladder that led upward.

"It goes to the playhouse," Penny said. "I remember. There's a trap door."

I started up the ladder. At the top I pushed hard, and a trap door eased upward. More darkness. I brought Penny up behind me, and we lit another match. We were in a small room, dark except for light shining beneath a door.

"This is the storeroom," Penny said. "That door opens into the big main room."

The light bothered me. Was someone in there? I didn't have time to worry about it. I eased open the door.

We entered a kind of dormitory. Bunk beds, blankets, dirty clothes, beer cans, overflowing ashtrays. This had to be where Butler's troops were bivouacked. But where were they? Out looking for us?

Suddenly a man emerged from another room, the bathroom, zipping up his fly. It was the black chauffeur. He reached for a gun, but I fired first. He doubled over. Penny screamed. I grabbed her hand, and we went running out into the darkness.

The hard rain slapped at our faces. Too late I realized I should have taken the man's gun. I was down to two shots. But by then we were running, away from the cabin, away from the lights of the mansion, toward the Sound. Why that way? Maybe I thought we'd find a boat there. Or maybe just because it was downhill, the path of least resistance.

"Down to the dock," I yelled.

I'd never known Penny could move so fast. But we kept slipping on the wet grass, and twice I crashed headlong into giant boxwoods. I lost Penny in darkness; then a bolt of lightning showed her twenty yards ahead of me. I caught up and yelled, "Stay together," but soon I had lost her again.

"Penny!" I yelled. "Where are you?"

I stopped and listened and heard the yelp of dogs behind me. Gasping for breath, I pushed on, and then I heard Penny scream. I thought she'd fallen, and I went stumbling through the rain and the darkness, calling her name, until another bolt of lightning split the heavens and revealed my most awful nightmare come true.

Nick Allegro held Penny before him, his forearm around her throat, a huge, ugly .45 automatic at her temple.

I was only ten feet from them. I pointed my gun at his head, cursing myself for not killing him before, knowing I couldn't be sure of hitting him and not her.

The lightning crashed again, and I saw his smirk, heard the words he bellowed through the rain.

"Drop it," he said.

"Don't do it, Daddy," she yelled. She groped for his eyes, but he jerked her head back, and I seemed to see his finger tighten on the trigger.

Maybe the best odds were to shoot him and hope for a miracle, but I couldn't do it, couldn't risk seeing her murdered before my eyes.

"Drop the gun," he yelled.

The dogs yelped behind us. The game was over; everything was over. I choked back a cry and tossed my revolver at his feet.

I heard Allegro laugh, and then I heard something else, a burst more loud and sudden than the lightning. Allegro's arms flew skyward; he shrieked once and crumpled to the ground.

Penny ran to me. There was blood in her hair, on her face, mixed with the rain. I didn't understand.

A shadow moved toward us from out of the storm. "Come on, Grady," he cried. It was Elton Capps, an Uzi machine gun in his hands. His long, ugly face looked quite deranged, but I could have kissed him.

"How did you find us?" I yelled.

"I know this place. The agency used it as a safe house for years. Come on."

"Where are we going?"

"I've got a boat. Dammit, let's go." He turned and started off, but I held back. Allegro's head was a truly awful sight. Penny gasped as I reached down and seized the dead man's automatic. Then we were running after Elton, toward the Sound.

We heard shouts behind us, and the yelp of dogs. We could see the pursuers, if only dimly, as an electrical storm raged above us, filling the sky with jagged light. Six or eight men were spread out across the lawn, moving inexorably toward us.

They opened fire as we neared the boathouse. It was built out over the water; we scrambled up the gangplank into our refuge, our port in the storm. Elton crouched by the door, firing at our pursuers, holding them off. I saw his rowboat tied at the end of the dock. As if reading my mind, he yelled, "It's no good now; we'd be sitting ducks."

I joined him at the door, peering out into the rain. "They're in those trees," he told me.

I studied the stand of pines fifty feet away and saw someone move. Slowly I leveled Allegro's big automatic at the shadow.

"Do you know how to use that thing?" Elton asked.

"I'm going to try."

"Go ahead. Just keep your head down."

I fired. I didn't hit anyone but firing the weapon made my blood run hot.

A burst from the trees raked the boathouse. I ducked, and Penny called, "Daddy, there's a speedboat here!"

We turned, and Elton cautiously shone his light to reveal a streamlined craft that was hoisted up on chains, six feet above the choppy waters.

"Does either of you know how to get it down?" Elton called.

"I do," Penny said. "A lifeguard used to take us on boat rides." She crept over and turned the switch that started the motor that lowered the boat. The motor caught, purred, and slowly, very slowly, the boat began to drop toward the dark water.

Elton, still crouched in the doorway, fired off a

round. "I can slow them down," he said. "But not forever."

The speedboat inched down. Penny found its keys hanging from a nail. But nothing could speed its descent; it hung by hooks that could not be released until it reached the water and began to float.

The men in the trees had stopped firing. I didn't know why, but it gave me hope.

The speedboat was a foot above the water. The chains holding it squeaked and groaned. More gunfire raked the boathouse. "Keep down, Penny," I yelled.

Suddenly, with a metallic thud, the boat stopped moving. "What's wrong?" Penny cried.

"They cut the electricity," Elton said.

He was crouched by the door, the Uzi clutched in his hands.

"Your rowboat," I said. "It's our only chance."

"It's no good. We wouldn't get ten feet."

"You take her," I said. "I'll hold them off."

Elton shook his head. "It won't work."

Just then there was a crash, a burst of flame at the far end of the boathouse. "A Molotov cocktail," Elton said.

I fired at a shadow down the beach. Perhaps I heard a cry of pain before it vanished.

"Let her take the boat, then," I pleaded. "Or for God's sake, maybe we can swim for it. This place is on fire. We've got to do something."

"No, Grady," Elton said. "I'm afraid it's time . . ."

A voice bellowed from outside. "Grady? This is Orth Butler. What are you doing? This is all a stupid mistake. Come out of there, and bring the others with you."

I strained to see him in the darkness; one shot was all I asked. "Yes, we're coming," Elton yelled back. "Hold your fire."

I didn't know what he meant—we were past bargaining or trickery—and I never found out, because abruptly a miracle exploded out of the night.

A new force was sweeping down the lawn from the house, shadows that fired as they came. There was something awesome about the speed and precision with which they moved, and Orth's men were quickly caught in a crossfire.

A firefight raged before our eyes. Orth's men were getting the worst of it—I heard them crying out—but before either side had won or lost, Elton said, "Come on, they've forgotten us, let's get out of here."

My instinct was different. "I think those are Uri's men," I said. "Let's wait and see what happens."

Elton seized my arm. "Dammit, man, he's part of the Sunrise scheme. They're fighting among themselves now, but whichever side wins wants you dead. We've got to get out while we can."

I let him persuade me. We didn't dare go ashore with the battle still raging, and the fire at the far end of the boathouse was starting to spread; the Sound seemed our only refuge. I told Penny what we were doing and helped her into the bow of the rowboat. "You row, Grady," he said, and I got into the middle of the boat and grabbed the oars. Elton climbed into the stern and pushed us away from the dock.

He was right about one thing. Nobody on the shore was thinking about us.

"Where shall I head?" I asked.

"Straight out," Elton said.

The worst of the storm had passed, but the rain was still falling. I rowed out fifty or sixty feet and stopped to rest. The little boat was being tossed about, and we were taking on water. "Now what?" I called.

"Farther," Elton said.

"How far out do you want to go?" I yelled back. "It's rough out here!"

Elton had been studying the battle that still raged on the shore. We could see flashes from automatic weapons, but it looked like Orth's men were in retreat.

He turned to me in anger. "Dammit, man, they may come after us in that speedboat. We've got to get out of sight; then we'll head back into shore. Just row on out!"

I rowed farther, until we were at least a hundred feet out at sea. Finally, Elton directed me toward a spit of land to the south. "My car's there," he explained.

The gunfire grew faint in the distance. Penny

rubbed the back of my neck. "You're doing great, Daddy," she whispered.

Elton said, "Grady, give me that damn gun before it falls out of your pocket and kills somebody."

I pulled in my oars, glad for a moment's rest, gave him the big automatic I had taken from Allegro, and started rowing again. My shoulders were starting to hurt, but I didn't care; it felt so damn good to finally be safe. It made sense that Elton would have saved us, a good friend, a brave man. I should have taken him to New York with me to start with. I laughed aloud; I'd never felt better in my life.

Then Penny cried, "Daddy!" and I looked up and saw that Elton had leveled the gun at my chest.

I stopped rowing and stared at his weathered Oklahoman face. "What are you doing, Elton?"

The storm had eased. The boat rocked uneasily, and it was terribly quiet out there, quiet and alone.

"Damn you, you pigheaded Irishman, I begged you to keep out of this. *Begged* you. But no, you had to be a hero. So here we are."

"Where?" I asked. "Where are we?"

"You and that idiot Prescott and that fool Butler may have blown Operation Sunrise, and if it's blown, a lot of good people will suffer."

"Agency people," I said, and it was not a question.

"Did they tell you it was *their* idea?" he asked scornfully.

"Elton, you've got me all wrong. All I want is to write my books. I don't give a damn about the Middle East."

"No, Grady, it won't wash. You're too stubborn, too filled with your bloody ideals. Orth wouldn't trust you, and I can't, either."

"What do you propose?"

"That you and the girl get into the water."

The girl, he called her. She had ridden in his fields, swum in his pond, taken him cookies when he was sick, and now he could calmly order her to her death. This was an Elton I had not known, not even suspected.

"Daddy, stop him!" Penny cried.

I was stalling, thinking fast. I could try to club him with an oar or make a dive for him, but he had the gun pointed at my heart, and he knew how to use it. He'd kill me before I moved two inches. Yet I might have to do that, hoping to turn over the boat, hoping Penny could escape.

"What happens when we get into the water?"

"It's cold and deep, Grady. It'll all be over in seconds. It's better than being shot. Linda will feel better about it."

He wanted our deaths to look accidental. That was what this whole charade had been about, saving us from the gunmen, maneuvering us into the boat, because drowning was more easily explained than gunshot wounds. And if we had any silly ideas about swimming, he'd be there to clobber us with an oar. This wasn't the perfect way to get rid of us—Uri's arrival must have upset his plan—but Elton was a professional; he could improvise.

I heard faint gunfire in the distance, but all that no longer mattered.

"Elton, you can trust me. Don't you think my daughter's life means more to me than—"

"Don't make it unpleasant," he said. "Not that it matters, but I regret this. Damn you, you've got the worst judgment of any man I ever met. Go on, Grady, get it over with."

I turned to speak to Penny, and as I did, my hand tightened on the oar. I wanted to tell her I loved her, then take one swing at the son of a bitch.

Before I could speak, a shot rang out.

Not Elton's shot.

Not mine.

Penny's.

God bless her, she plugged him between the eyes, the way they always do. Elton grunted, then slumped forward and died at my feet. Penny threw her arms around me, trembling, sobbing, but tears were a luxury now. We were drifting out to sea. I thought for a moment and started rowing back toward the burning boathouse at Sleepy Harbor.

Penny was still clutching my Saturday night special.

"Where'd you get it?" I asked. I was confused, dazed.

"Nick made you throw it on the ground, remember? And when you picked up his gun, I grabbed yours. It seemed like the thing to do."

Too much was happening. I wondered if I should throw Elton's body overboard, but I couldn't bring myself to touch him. "Listen, Penny, forget the whole thing. I shot him."

I grabbed my little gun from her, wiped it clean of fingerprints, and tossed it into the sea. I still had Allegro's automatic, and Elton's Uzi, if I could figure how to fire the damn thing.

We were fifty feet out from the burning boat-house; shadowy figures were running along the shoreline.

"Malloy, is that you?" a man called.

I pulled in my oars, pointed the Uzi at him, waited.

"It's Uri," the man shouted. "Come in."

Penny hugged me. "Daddy, who is it? Do you trust him?"

I thought about it. "I'm not sure," I said, and began rowing toward the shore.

Uri waded out to meet me, his hands high to show he was unarmed. When he reached us, Penny was crying—how could she know who he was? I kept the gun pointed at his chest. "Can I trust you?"

"You have to," he said.

He took the Uzi from me. Four of his commandos pulled our rowboat onto the sand and helped us out.

Uri looked at the body slumped at my feet. "So Elton beat me here," he said.

"You've met?"

"We were allies at times. He was a talented man."

"He liked you, too," I said.

Uri smiled briefly. "We must leave at once. Orth Butler is dead. The police are no doubt on the way. There are a great many explanations to be made, and Senator Prescott is best qualified to make them."

I couldn't argue with that. Uri took my arm, and Penny's, too, and helped us up the long lawn toward the mansion. His men fanned out around us, their automatic weapons cradled in their arms. The house was dark and quiet. I guessed Harry was in there, on the phone, maybe, talking to his advisers, dreaming up an explanation for the carnage. I didn't doubt that he'd come up with one.

Their cars were parked in the trees near the mansion. Penny and Uri and I climbed in the back of one of them, with two of his young men up front. Penny huddled against me, too tired to pay attention to these broad-shouldered, dark-eyed young warriors. Thank God for small favors. As we pulled away, I looked back in wonder at the burning boathouse and, past it, the first pink kiss of dawn.

29

I skipped Orth Butler's funeral, but the rest of the world was there. The *Washington Post* carried a picture of the front two rows of mourners at the National Cathedral. Harry and Amanda and Bonnie were up front, of course (Harry looking grave, Amanda fashionable, Bonnie dazed), along with the president and vice-president and the first and second ladies. The second row was jam-packed with ex-presidents and ex-secretaries of state, all come to honor "this great and good American who had been tragically taken from us," as the vice-president orated.

The official story was that Orth was shot by PLO terrorists. That was preposterous enough to be believed and helped account for the night's carnage. Elton wasn't among the Sleepy Harbor dead, however; his body turned up in an alley in Brooklyn a couple of days later, a mystery that, God willing, may never be solved.

Orth's death gave Harry a good excuse to put off

his announcement a few more months. Lucky Harry, everything was breaking his way. Other candidates kept self-destructing and as a noncandidate Harry continued to receive great press. One of the newsmagazines carried a flattering cover story with pictures of him and Amanda and Bonnie and much talk of what a "close-knit family" they are.

Harry called the day after Orth's funeral and asked if he could come see me. "Come alone," I told him.

Linda and I argued about it. She said if she saw Harry Prescott she might kill him. Nice talk. There'd been enough killing. So I saw Harry alone.

He accepted a beer, and we settled before the fire in my study. He looked young and vigorous in jeans, boots, a plaid shirt, and an old tweed coat, as if Orth's death had lifted a great weight from his shoulders.

"I'll announce just after Super Tuesday," he began. "It looks good. No cakewalk, but a good shot. The money's there. The party's fragmented and desperate for leadership."

When I didn't say anything, he added, "I still want you on my team."

"I've got a book to write."

Harry sipped his beer before he spoke. "Grady, the Sunrise plan died with Orth. He pushed me into it— You didn't think I'd go through with it, did you, once I was president? My God, the man was mad. But now I'll be able to do great things. Disarmament? The

284

moment is perfect." A pause, a lowering of his voice. "I need you."

Stirring words, but my patience was wearing thin.

"Harry, let me refresh your memory. Orth did his damnedest to kill me and my daughter the other night because we knew about your nutty scheme, and you didn't lift a hand to stop him. Okay, maybe your scheme is dead. Maybe you don't want to kill us anymore. But I can't be sure of that."

"Jesus, Grady, do you—?"

"Shut up and listen. I've written down everything I know. I gave sealed copies to two reporters, to be opened in case I die or disappear. As long as I'm healthy, you're still a great American. But if I check out, you'll have a lot of explaining to do, whether you're the candidate or president or whatever. Do you understand?"

Damn him, he started laughing. He laughed and laughed and finally said, "You have everything wrong. Nobody wanted to kill you. We wanted to *talk* to you, for Pete's sake. And you went running through the night shooting at people. Look, you're a great writer, but good God, you *do* let your imagination run amok sometimes."

He kept chuckling and finished his beer and stood up. "Look, you've been under a strain; you need a rest, fine. But later on, when you're up to snuff, come see me. I'll always have a place for you."

Harry was smiling as he left, as well he might be.

What could be more perfect for him than for me to voluntarily shut up? Linda was livid when I told her what I'd done; she wanted to kill him or, failing that, for me to go to the FBI. But she had more faith in the wheels of justice than I did. And, for that matter, what did I know? The tape was destroyed, Orth and Elton were dead, and Harry's PR men would paint me as a nutty writer with a grudge.

Besides, any investigation would in time get to Elton's death, and Harry's people would spread the word that Elton was last seen alive with me and Penny in a rowboat. I couldn't put her through that ordeal, and Harry knew I couldn't. Even if I said I shot Elton, it would undercut my credibility; at worst, I might wind up on trial for murder. It's hard to win a pissing contest with a U.S. senator, much less with the White House. I had a wild story about a dead tycoon and Arab oil fields and World War III, but Harry had prestige and PR men and plausibility on his side. There was a good chance that if I tried to tell the world the truth, I'd end up in jail, and Harry would be president nonetheless.

The real question was whether Operation Sunrise died with Orth and Elton. To put it another way, was it possible that Harry was telling the truth? For what it's worth, there was an item in the papers a week after the shootings reporting the resignations of the deputy chief of Israeli intelligence and one of their top defense ministers. I'd told Uri everything I knew, and

I took this to mean he'd gone back and shot down the faction that was trying to involve the Israeli government in the Sunrise scheme.

But what about the Russians? Orth had some sort of deal with them; did Harry still have the same understanding? And what about the CIA? I now thought that the whole business of Elton's writing a book and being denounced by the agency was a scheme to distance him from them, to create a deep cover while he pursued Operation Sunrise. I had seen Harry as Orth's front, but now I began to wonder if Orth was Elton's front—if the CIA, or elements of it, was behind the entire scheme. If so, it wouldn't die with Elton.

There was a lot about Elton's role that I would never understand. I think he was truly upset when I blundered into Operation Sunrise and tried to steer me away from it. But finally he decided that Orth and his hired gun, Nick Allegro, were screwing up my case and he'd have to take charge personally. So he came to Sleepy Harbor to supervise my accidental death, but by then Penny and I were on the run. He found us, killed the blundering Allegro when he got the chance, and maneuvered me and Penny into a boat to stage our drowning, but Uri arrived in time to save us.

But did Operation Sunrise live on somewhere deep in the bowels of the CIA? If so, there were patriots there who wished me dead—in the name of world peace, of course. What I had told Harry about giving sealed envelopes to two reporters was true. But was that enough insurance? If you thought about it, did it really matter what I said? If one day there was war in the Middle East and a U.S.-Soviet raid on the oil fields, would anyone give a damn if some writer said it was all part of a plot?

I didn't know. I went back to living my life. Penny's in her second semester now and has a steady boyfriend, so we don't receive daily bulletins from the front anymore. I inquire often about the boy's health. Before she went back to school, I persuaded her it was best if she forgot what she heard on the tape and the gory events at Sleepy Harbor. I persuaded Linda, too, more or less. And so peace returned to our little world—the winter snows, the spring thaw, true happiness.

Penny called the other day with an update on Bonnie. She's hit her parents for a generous allowance (actually, she inherited twenty million dollars from Orth but doesn't get anything until she's twenty-one), and now she's living with Mario in the Village. She's attending art school, and he's working in his parents' restaurant and taking courses at NYU. Mario's a tough kid, and he'll be good for her; it looks like he and she have already struck a hard bargain for her silence. Penny said Bonnie wants me to come to dinner the next time I'm in New York, but I think I'll let that one slide a few years.

Harry finally announced, and his prospects look

good. Our party is in its usual disarray, and a lot of people think he'll be nominated on the first ballot. The other night I watched Barbara Walters interview him, and it struck me, suddenly and absolutely, that this rich, handsome, well-informed, supremely confident man almost certainly will be president.

Harry has a quality, a magic, on television, that I'd not appreciated before. He sits there and talks and smiles and makes self-effacing jokes and looks concerned as hell about the rest of us; somehow, as you watch, he makes you feel *good*. God help me, knowing all that I know, I watched him for ten minutes, and I was grinning like a loon.

It occurred to me as I watched him that, like Ruth in her candlelit brownstone, like me at my word processor, Harry, too, is in the pleasure business, and on a more cosmic scale than anything Ruth or I could imagine. She dealt in flesh, and I in words, but Harry deals in dreams, and dreams are the ultimate pleasure. He comes into our homes and speaks sweet words and tells us our dreams can come true, that we can have peace in our time, and justice and equality and opportunity and all those other lofty intangibles we crave. That's all most of us want—not a job or a handout, just the warm glow of our illusions—and Harry delivers, and that's why he'll be president.

Watching Harry that day, I began to think that the question was not could I stop him—for I still thought of that—but did I want to stop him?

I'm on speaking terms with most of the other candidates in the race, and even knowing about Operation Sunrise, I can't say that I'm sure they'd be any better than Harry. Does that sound cynical? Perhaps that depends on how old you are, how many campaigns you've been through.

You come to Washington young, filled with high hopes, and in time you learn that politics is a choice between lesser evils, nothing more. No one understood that better than those very tough, sophisticated men who started our nation. Harry is, for me at least, a known quantity—a known evil, if you wish—and if he wins the nomination, I'll almost certainly consider him a lesser evil than whomever the other party puts up.

Harry's chief rival in our party simply isn't very smart—we've had enough dunces in the White House for a while—and one of the chief contenders in the other party is a man I truly fear would blow up the world.

So I won't blow the whistle on Harry. Maybe, after the convention, if he's nominated, I'll climb aboard the campaign plane and let fly with a little rhetoric. It's something I'm good at—the leap from writing fiction to writing political speeches is not all that great—and it's a hell of a way to see America.

Perhaps, if I was there at his side, I could keep an eye on him, nudge him now and then in the right direction. That, at least, is part of the fantasy.

Am I rationalizing? Am I cynical? Perhaps. But I enjoy politics, and if Harry makes it to the White House, I might do a little good in the world.

God knows the world could use it.

What the hell, I'm in the pleasure business.